Despair

André Alexis

Despair

AND OTHER STORIES

HENRY HOLT AND COMPANY · NEW YORK

Henry Holt and Company, LLC
Publishers since 1866
115 West 18th Street
New York, New York 10011

Henry Holt ® is a registered trademark of
Henry Holt and Company, LLC.

Originally published in 1994 in Canada
by Coach House Press

Library of Congress Cataloging-in-Publication Data
Alexis, André, 1957–
Despair and other stories / André Alexis.—1st American ed.
p.   cm.
ISBN 0-8050-5979-2 (alk. paper)
1. Ottawa (Ont.)—Social life and customs—Fiction. 2. Trinidad—Social life
and customs—Fiction. 3. Trinidadians—Ontario—Ottawa—Fiction. I. Title.
PR9199.3.A365D47   1999   98-41602
813'.54—dc21   CIP

Henry Holt books are available for special promotions and
premiums. For details contact: Director, Special Markets.

First American Edition 1999

Printed in the United States of America

1 3 5 7 9 10 8 6 4 2

To
Adrina Ena Borde
Nicola Ena Alexis-Brooks

CONTENTS

·I·

Michael

The Night Piece

1.

It had been a beautiful wedding.

Even Michael's father had managed a smile. He had risen and fallen with everyone else as they rose and fell in prayer. Father Albert hadn't gone on too long: a few words about connubial bliss, a prayer to the God of light, and a passage from the Song of Solomon. Michael's mother had cried quietly, then the bells had pealed, the new order was heralded, and sin was banished to those unfortunate beds that were neither bridal nor conjugal.

Inside, the church was quiet. Light pierced the stained-glass windows, touching the outermost pews, leaving the congregation in shadow. The stillness smelled of incense and talcum powder, wood and rose water. The statue of the Virgin, her bare foot on the serpent's head, was graceful in its alcove.

Outside, the sun was bright. The church steps had been swept, the black railings polished, and the rectangles of lawn cut.

But for the cars and trucks that rumbled by, the scene was idyllic.

Now the question was: who would go with whom to the Botanical Gardens?

A few of the guests had no idea where the gardens were. Others hadn't the means to get there. So it was some time before directions were given and transportation arranged. The wedding ended at noon, but it was two o'clock before everyone scattered.

And again an hour before the reception began.

For Michael, age fifteen, it was the same mysterious thing as every gathering: all of these people, family or friends of family, whom you rarely saw. Better they had been total strangers. That way, there would be no taps on the head, no big kisses, no tearful "Remember me?"s. (Those were the worst. You looked into tired old faces, into the eyes of men and women who had cleaned your shit-stained bum or suffered you to vomit on their shoulders. Of course they remembered you, but why should you remember them?)

The reception hall was an immense rectangle. Twenty long tables were strategically placed to allow for a stage and, between the stage and the guests, a dance floor.

Michael sat beside his mother at a table near the center of the hall. The food was Trinidadian, or most of it was. They began with a hot fish soup, and then there was chicken roti, pelau, crab and callaloo, sugar cake, and sweet bread. It was all very good, but it was gone as quickly as it had come.

The meal was over in minutes, and before it could be digested the groom's brother climbed on stage and told off-color jokes, which he read surreptitiously from small white cue cards.

That went on forever. Michael counted ten cue cards before he lost track, and when the jokes were over there were speeches: speeches from the father of the bride and the mother of the bride, the sister of the groom and the mother of the groom, a friend of the groom and a friend of the bride, an honored guest from Curepe, and then, finally, a tired old man from Belmont who forgot what it was he had come to say. It was six o'clock before the music started and they were free to move.

When the dancing began, Michael got up and wandered. He went from table to table, stopping here to sit with his uncle Horace, or there to talk to an adult who called him over:

—You look so much like your father, they said. (or)

—You look so much like your mother!

And then they let him go. (Like a fish.)

It was as he moved away from a group of reminiscing relations that Michael noticed a young man sitting alone at a table. He was thin, and his skin was a peculiar color: brown beneath a translucent layer of gray, the color of long illness or long convalescence. The man coughed, looked up at Michael, turned away.

The music was loud. Sparrow sang:

—One a de women started to beg. He bite she on she chest. He bite she on she leg . . .

And everyone sang along:

—I envy de Congo man . . .

It was a song Michael couldn't understand. He began to feel uncomfortable in the midst of so many people. So he went out through the kitchen.

Outside, the sun was setting. The midges had already begun to pester the outdoor lights, and the moon was up in the evening sky. There was a cool breeze, and the earth smelled damp. (At that moment Michael felt, from the bottom of his fifteen years, that this sky, the way the world felt this evening, this was his fate: to be outside and alone, unable to say "I'm outside and alone" but able to bear it, because it was his fate.) A voice beside him said:

—The thing I'll miss, it's the sky. The sky, then the sun. I'll miss the earth, the way it looks now, but mostly the sky . . . and the river . . .

It was the thin young man. He was even more emaciated, like a flattened straw, in this light. There was only his gray suit to give him bulk.

—I'm sorry . . . , he said. My name's Winston Grant.

Without thinking, Michael asked:

—Are you ill?

—No, Winston answered. I'm dying.

And he looked up at the night sky.

What does he mean? Michael thought as he watched Winston try to light a cigarette. The man's hands shook like twigs.

—I must look awful, Winston said.

But he wasn't upset.

2.

It was complicated.

First, he wasn't as old as he looked. He was twenty-one. (At twenty he'd been in good health and his breath hadn't been quite so bad.) His decline began with an ad in the *Citizen*:

Wanted: Man about the house for elderly woman. Room and board. Generous wages. Trinidadian preferred. Call (613) 588-6180.

It was meant for him. He'd been looking for work since leaving his parents' home. He was a diligent worker. He enjoyed the company of the elderly, and although he'd lived most of his life in Canada, he was Trinidadian by birth.

And he was perfect. The elderly woman, Mrs. Fernandez by name, hired him on the spot, without an elaborate interview and with few questions about his origin. In fact, after pinching both his arms above the elbow and both his legs above the knees (to make certain they weren't wooden), her only personal question had been:

—Are you a light sleeper?

—Not really, Winston answered.

—Good, she said. I have mice in the walls.

The mice weren't the only trouble with the house. It was a slightly run-down, two-story building of brick and wood in Sandy Hill, not much worse than the places around it but still remarkable. The gardens in front and back were unkempt. The porch needed painting. The windows were ancient and their panes were lumpy.

Inside there was the same sort of disrepair, but to somewhat different effect. White candles were left on tables and ledges. The wooden floors were covered with bright, handmade rugs into which were woven eccentric designs. The walls downstairs were spotless, but on the second floor they were dirty and, in the rooms he was shown, brightly colored images had been painted on them.

The house was disheveled but comfortable.

Winston's room was a large rectangle in which there was a bed, a night table, and a chair. On the table were a ewer and a bowl, and a young woman without eyes (or, more precisely, without irises) was painted on the wall.

—This is your room, said Mrs. Fernandez. Mines is quite over there at the other end of the house. I like to go to sleep at nine o'clock, so try to be restful . . .

She touched the painting on the wall.

—I must finish this one, she said.

It was Winston's duty to take care of the house. This meant cutting the lawn, painting the front porch and the wooden trim, cleaning the eaves, washing the windows, repairing the roof, and pulling weeds from the garden. He was also expected to work inside, to sweep the floors, help Mrs. Fernandez with the walls, and put the basement in order. (The basement was a calling of its own: a dark, low-ceilinged set of rooms into which Winston went with trepidation. Hundreds of glass jars filled with jellies and liquids had been left about, and the dirt was a second skin on the walls.)

Needless to say, there was little time for anything but work.

Winston spent his first week cutting the lawn and painting the house. He met Mrs. Munro, one of the next-door neighbors, and learned to avoid her. She was an elderly, red-haired woman, loquacious to a fault, who called him over whenever she caught his attention, to show off photographs of her blond and freckled grandchildren. She would then go on and on about anything at all: her late husband, the state of her lawn, the way her windows let the sunlight in . . .

—You know, Winston, these mosquitoes are biting the hell out of me, like it was something personal . . . I can't sleep for slapping . . . slapping . . .

And so on, until it got dark or until you moved out of the range of her voice. (Mrs. Fernandez never spoke to Mrs. Munro and warned Winston about her:

—Keep your head down when you see she coming, she said.)

In the evening he would stay indoors and help Mrs. Fernandez wash the dishes or clean the walls, sweep the floors or move the furniture about. In this way, he came to know her well.

She was terrified of salt and swore she could smell it on his breath whenever he ate elsewhere. She had a thing about the walls downstairs. She kept them clean as a whistle.

While doing the walls, she liked to have passages read to her from the Bible, the only book that held her interest.

She wore the same clothes day in and day out: pink slippers, thick nylon stockings (for her varicose veins), a blue summer dress, and a white scarf to keep her white hair in place.

After a while, it was clear they would get along. Even though Mrs. Fernandez worked him like a dog, Winston felt at home. She cooked his meals and watched him eat. ("You don't mind about the salt, eh, Winston? It isn't good for you.") She was kind. She coaxed him into conversation (and so discovered, after all, that his parents lived in Blossom Park, that although he *was* of Trinidadian origin he was Canadian as could be). It was as though he'd been adopted.

The only company she received came, without fail, on Sunday mornings before mass. Older men and women brought her presents: clothes, which she used to clean the walls; food, which she watched Winston eat; and bottles of a liquid, which she kept in the basement.

The guests came in groups of four or five, and they invariably treated Winston with respect. They bowed or kissed his hands or put his hands to their face or touched his face, but none of them ever spoke to him directly. The closest he came to a conversation was one Sunday when an extremely old woman said:

—Isn't it a lovely day?

At the sound of these words, the people with her

froze. They were all on the front steps to the house, as friendly a place as Winston knew, but it was as if they were frightened. They kept smiling, looking down at their feet, as though nothing had been said. Winston answered:

—It's a beautiful day.

And Mrs. Fernandez came up behind him.

—Isn't it? she said. Did someone speak to you just now, Winston?

The woman who had spoken was clearly senile. She looked happily up at the sky while her companions stood in place, leaning away from her. Winston answered:

—No.

And immediately the guests were calm. They entered, left their presents, and went out again as soon as it was polite. They touched his face as they departed, but none of them spoke.

Winston did work hard, but he was well paid, and in theory, his weekends were his own.

During the first months, his life continued on the same course: he visited his parents or stayed with friends on his days off, drinking until three in the morning or watching foreign films with Adele, a friend from Carleton. Gradually, though, he lost interest in the world outside of Mrs. Fernandez's house. After six months with her, he felt too tired to make the trip to Blossom Park, too tired to stay out all night, too tired to watch movies that didn't make sense.

Maybe he worked too hard. He lost weight. He felt

physically uncomfortable. His back and the backs of his legs were itchy, as if there were boils beneath his shoulder blades and mosquito bites behind his knees. His body felt as though it had been wrung out to dry. His mind drifted into a peculiar loop: he couldn't stop thinking about scissors, broken glass, beetles, and garden loam. Sometimes it was beetles in loam, sometimes beetles in glass. Then it was scissors in loam or scissors in glass or beetles on scissors . . . He began to feel unhappy with the work he did for Mrs. Fernandez.

Still, she was not unhappy with him. She was pleased to pay his wages, and she was genuinely depressed on his days off.

—Winston, I know is your day off, but stay around the house. What if I need you?

And she became a little too familiar, patting his stomach and letting her hand linger, rubbing his head and touching his face. (What did these people want with his face?) As though their relations had become courtship, you might almost have said Mrs. Fernandez was infatuated. Isn't that why she sometimes entered the bathroom while he showered?

—Winston? I come to change the towels.

When he wasn't thinking about scissors or mirrors, he thought about that.

What was she up to? Did she sleep at night? (He certainly did. There were times he fell asleep at the dinner table, or in the living room, and he had dim memories of Mrs. Fernandez, old and frail as she was, dragging him up to bed.) What if she did things to him without his knowing? Should he be upset? Flattered? Disgusted? No, angry is what he would be. It was the principle: you weren't supposed to touch people at night without their consent. Of course, he hadn't had anything like sexual cooperation in so long, it was possible the rules had changed . . . No. Sex with Mrs. Fernandez wouldn't be sex at all. It would be more like filial excess.

—What's that about excess, Winston?

He'd been speaking aloud without realizing it.

—You're not eating, Mrs. Fernandez said. Eat . . .

He took a mouthful of pigeon peas. They were bitter. He would normally have swallowed and gone on to the chicken, but tonight he spat quietly into his left hand, put his hand beneath the table, and crushed the partially eaten peas in a ridge on the underside of the tabletop. Mrs. Fernandez didn't notice, but she was surprised at how quickly he'd finished them. He said:

—I'm so tired.

And she smiled, insisted on helping him up to bed.

She had the grip of a sailor. Holding him by the waist, pulling his arm around her shoulder, she didn't even notice his resistance. In his room, she let his body fall to the bed like a sack of rice. Immediately, she began to undress him.

—What are you doing? he asked.

—You still awake? Well, take off your clothes and sleep.

It was only seven o'clock, but that is more or less what he did. He slept for an hour and was woken by the sound of a door clacking shut. He was convinced it was morning, but no, the luminous numbers on his alarm clock said eight, and it was dark outside. He'd been dreaming of mason jars filled with topsoil: a soothing dream, until the jars broke. He'd had a box of straight pins with which to catch the insects that scuttered from the jars, and each time he thought he'd managed to pin one of the beetles down he pierced his own fingers.

From eight until midnight, he lay in bed, bone-tired, drifting in and out of sleep. (At nine o'clock, Mrs. Fernandez retired for the night. He heard the *click* of her door closing, then silence.) He thought about his future: how long could he endure a travail that left him so depleted? It's true Mrs. Fernandez paid him well, but after six months he'd managed to spend so little: a white blouse for his mother, a leather tie for his father, a book on Coleridge for Adele . . .

It was winter and the moonlight came through his bedroom window to touch the face on the wall, the eyeless young woman. It was a disconcerting image, not a scene you wanted to enter. Still, there was something seductive about it, and he fell into a light sleep thinking about Adele's shoulders.

At midnight, Winston was woken by an unbearable silence. The moonlight still fell against his wall, his room was unchanged, but the house was different. There was a light on in the hall outside his door, and then he heard footsteps. Thinking it was Mrs. Fernandez coming to molest him, he said:

—So, it's true . . .

But it wasn't true in the way he imagined.

A woman entered his bedroom, but it wasn't Mrs. Fernandez. From what he could see, she was young and beautiful. She was also naked, but so at ease it was as if she were clothed. She needed no light to find Winston, turn him onto his stomach, pull up his shirt, and pull down his pajama pants. Then, after a slight hesitation to suck her teeth, she bit his back beneath both shoulder blades, and the soft flesh behind both of his knees.

And what did Winston do during all this? Nothing. Nothing at all. He could barely move. She held his head down with one hand while the other kept his nates in place. Then, when she bit the underside of his knees, she kept a hand on his nates and another on his ankles. In any case, it was quickly over. She left the room, casually pulling the door behind her.

Frightened, Winston put his hands on the back of his legs where she'd bitten: there was blood, but very little. He sat up and listened for the sound of her footsteps: she was somewhere downstairs. It occurred to him that he was dreaming, and no sooner did he think it than he was convinced. Yes, the young woman looked familiar; the situation was ludicrous but terrifying. It was a dream. He would get up and go downstairs for milk.

He did get up, though he felt faint and his thoughts were confused. (For instance, he couldn't remember who he was, and he couldn't decide what difference it made, though he knew it should have made some.) Once outside his room, he saw that Mrs. Fernandez's door was open and her lights were on.

—If she's downstairs, she can't be upstairs, Winston thought.

So he went quietly to her bedroom.

Save for one detail, it was as he'd expected. The room smelled of an exotic and insistent potpourri. The walls were bare and white, and there was little furniture: a chest of drawers, on top of which was a variety of phials, vials, and bottles; a straight-backed wooden chair; a night table; and a plain, narrow cot.

The exceptional detail was Mrs. Fernandez herself: she lay fully dressed on top of the cot, her shoes hanging off her feet, which were themselves hanging over the edge of the bed. Her eyes were open; she was staring at the ceiling.

When he saw her, Winston jumped. His mind raced through hundreds of apologies in a millisecond: I'm sorry, I'm so sorry, jeez I'm sorry . . .

—I'm . . . , he said.

Before he realized there was something wrong: Mrs. Fernandez wasn't breathing. Her body was as flat as if it had been pressed in a Chinese laundry.

Hoping it was all a trick of the light, Winston spoke up.

—Mrs. Fernandez! he said in a loud whisper.

No answer.

He approached and, lifting her arm, saw that she was indeed flat, lifeless, a Mrs. Fernandez costume of flesh and skin. Now he was even more frightened. He held her flat hand as if it were a dead mouse. A woman's voice said:

—Is like yuh want to fock de old lady.

And Winston cried out in surprise. His heart stammered, and for only the sixth time in his life, he lost consciousness.

3.

It was even more complicated.

Until Mrs. Fernandez, Winston's life had been tolerable. He had his complement of friends, acquaintances, and strangers known by sight alone. He shared the aspirations of those around him. He loved his parents, and he was almost at ease in the country to which they'd come.

So why was he in this particular nightmare?

The morning after he discovered the flat body of Mrs. Fernandez, Winston awoke in his own bed. Sitting beside him, staring into his eyes, was Mrs. Fernandez. She looked neither friendly nor unfriendly; her face was impassive.

—Good morning, she said.

—Good morning, he answered.

—You didn't hear anything last night?

—No.

Her eyes were a diluted brown.

—I didn't sleep well at all, she said. It was like someone in me bedroom . . .

—I didn't hear anything . . . I'm so tired these days . . .

Mrs. Fernandez smiled slightly, and Winston knew she'd been spiking his food.

—Oho, she said. I just wondered if you hear anything.

Then she got up from the side of his bed and waddled slowly out.

At the *click* of the door, Winston lay back, his neck on his pillow. Mrs. Fernandez was maternal again. She was unlike the flesh she'd been the night before, but he knew what she was. He was incredulous, of course. Who would expect to find a Soucouyant here, in this place, so far from where they usually apportioned death?

Now, let's see . . . if Mrs. Fernandez *was* a Soucouyant, the problem was this: how to rub salt in her skin. That's how the story went, wasn't it? To kill a Soucouyant, you rubbed the inside of her skin with salt, and that would do it. Her nasty self, unable to return to its hiding place, died.

It was ridiculous. But say, for argument's sake, it was true. Mrs. Fernandez could smell salt a mile away. How would he bring it into the house?

He lay in bed, vaguely plotting a course of action: first, he would approach Mrs. Munro. She would have salt. He would ask her for a cupful. She would go on about her husband, poor dead soul, but she would give him the salt. He would keep it in a plastic bag, in his pants pocket. Then, at night, he would hunt the creature down and rub the salt in her skin . . . Really, it was just like his parents and their friends to bring a death so bizarre with them from Trinidad . . .

—Winston? You ain' getting up for work?

Still, wasn't it easier to believe in a vivid dream than it was to admit that your employer sucked your blood while you slept? And there were so many questions: how had he gotten back to his own room? Mrs. Fernandez might have dragged him, but then why the questions about his sleep? He *did* feel the bites beneath his shoulder blades and behind his knees, but what did that prove? Maybe the bedbugs were resourceful. There *was* something in his food, and he did object to being drugged, but maybe Mrs. Fernandez was solicitous of his sleep. That seemed more likely than that she wanted his blood . . .

—Winston! Get up nah man . . .

That day, he shoveled snow from the front walk. He shoveled snow from the patio stones. He climbed to the roof and shoveled snow from its shingles. It was a day for fires and soft rugs. His breath hung before him like pot handles, and by the time he came in for the evening he was exhausted and hungry.

It took all of his will to leave the food Mrs. Fernandez put before him: grouper soup, stewed chicken and rice, callaloo, Mauby. He asked for very little, and whenever she turned away he put fistfuls of chicken and rice into the pockets of his winter coat, which hung on the back of his chair. He felt ridiculous.

That night, as before, the moon shone down on the

portrait of the young woman. He heard Mrs. Fernandez
retire around nine o'clock (*click*), and he drifted in and
out of sleep. And again, near midnight, he was woken
by the silence, and she came in, turned him summarily
on his stomach, and bit him beneath the shoulder
blades and behind the knees.

When she'd finished, the Soucouyant turned him
back as he'd been, face toward the ceiling. She sat on the
end of his bed, her cold hands holding his ankles down.

—Open you eyes nah man. Ah could see you's
awake . . . Dat is de problem wit' allayuh koonoo-
moonoo. Is like yuh t'ink you so smart . . .

Despite feeling weak and afraid, Winston was awake
until just before dawn. That he and the Soucouyant
spoke at all was baffling when he thought about it later,
but speak they did. She had a deep voice and the per-
sonality of a brushfire, but he was seduced by her complete attention to everything he said. She stared at his
face. She watched his lips move. She asked about
his family. So, although he was frightened, he found it
easier and easier to answer her questions as the night
went on. He didn't relax, exactly, but he stopped fear-
ing for his life. Besides, she was beautiful to him, and
she was unclothed.

The Soucouyant had long, dark hair, almond-shaped
eyes, a nose that was a trifle broad, full lips, and a
strong chin. Her neck was graceful, her breasts full, her
hips narrow. Were it not for her breath, she was his
imagined ideal of a brown-skinned woman. (But she

was nothing of the sort. She was neither beautiful nor attentive. Her hair was not soft, nor were her breasts full. "She" was not a woman, after all.)

Sometime near dawn, when the light in his room turned blue, the Soucouyant released his ankles. Winston was so exhausted he fell asleep almost immediately. She went out the door and he heard her footsteps going off, but her steps became part of a soothing dream and he couldn't tell which way she'd gone.

It seemed as if he'd slept for no more than a few seconds when Mrs. Fernandez shook him awake.

—Good morning, she said.

But it wasn't morning. Outside, the light was blinding. The sun shone on the white world: noon, at the earliest. Mrs. Fernandez stared at his face.

—You ain' getting up for work?

In the weeks that followed, Winston did get up and he did work, but it was as if competing impulses governed him. During the day Mrs. Fernandez kept him shoveling, digging, and sweeping, but as he swept, shoveled, and dug he feverishly sought a means of escape. He meditated on the Soucouyant's death. Where did she keep her skin now that he knew what she was? Where could he hide salt? Could he bring himself to obliterate her?

At night, the Soucouyant took over his imagination. Though she only touched his ankles and her hands were always cold, he was convinced that she wanted to do more, that she wanted to caress him, that her touch was warm, and all he desired in the world was to put his head on her shoulder and tell her how lonely he'd been. (And it really did seem as if he'd been lonely without her.)

The weeks turned to months and each month saw an escalation of the conflict within: his desire for the Soucouyant deepened, as did his desperation to be rid of her, but he grew less and less able to think of anyone else. Even Mrs. Fernandez seemed to drift in and out of his consciousness: here she was looking into his eyes after his nights with the Soucouyant; there she was pointing to this or that corner of the property that needed attention: the garden, the front walk, the roof, or again: the kitchen, the dining room, the basement.

Naturally, it wasn't long before Winston's health deteriorated. (No, he *wasn't* ill. His condition had no name, unless you count *mal de pays*.) He ate sparingly, taking small mouthfuls of what he imagined were "safe" foods: carrots, lettuce, potatoes, and cabbage. And then he stopped eating altogether.

Mrs. Fernandez would say:

—You're getting very skinny.

And he would answer:

—I just don't feel hungry.

And it was true. He'd stopped feeling hungry.

And then, one morning, Mrs. Fernandez woke him from sleep when the daylight was still blue. In her lap was a red porcelain bowl filled with black beetles. With one hand, she held his mouth open; with the other, she pushed the beetles in.

—You mus' eat, she said.

He hadn't eaten for weeks, and he was so tired he swallowed without resistance, distracted only by the flesh of her thumb pushing up against his teeth. Perhaps it *was* Mrs. Fernandez's way of keeping her prey alive, but she was so maternal in her ministrations that he ate the beetles without distress. It was a turning point in their relationship.

Now Winston became someone else, as if a self he'd always harbored finally pushed him aside. He lost track of his days entirely. Night after night, he listened to the sound of his own voice. Aroused by her beauty, trying to accept her stench, he lost his will to destroy the Soucouyant. (It seemed uncharitable to rub salt in her skin.)

Gradually, she came to accept his submission. She relaxed her cold grip on his ankles. She allowed him to come as close to her as he could before the smell defeated him. (She also allowed him to turn his back to her, to offer up his shoulders and knees—which he did, as if it were a sacred act.) And so, what had begun as resistance became, for Winston, affection, affection and desire, affection and longing.

Really, but for the niggling voice of his own death, a voice like hearing a shadow speak, you could call it love . . .

Winston's hands shook, but he managed to light a cigarette.

Above them, the sky had darkened; the stars were bright. It was a quiet evening until, all of a sudden, the wedding returned: a song by Kitch, laughter, the pounding of feet on the dance floor, and Michael's name being called. And then, his uncle Horace was beside them.

—You out here? he asked Michael. Come inside . . .

And, seeing Winston:

—Winston, good evening.

And again, to Michael:

—Come inside. Your father wants you for a picture.

And he was gone, taking the wedding with him when he closed the door.

He had broken the connection between the young men. Winston looked up at the moon and let the cigarette smoke escape from his lungs.

—Anyway, he said, I'm dying, but I'm not sick.

He was lying. Michael knew it for certain.

—What happened to Mrs. Munro? he asked.

—Who? The neighbor? Nothing happened.

—You don't look so weak . . .

(He did, though.)

—So why are you dying?

—It doesn't have a name, said Winston.

It wasn't true. It was a lie, and even if it was true it was impossible, and if it was impossible it couldn't be true . . . It was as though Michael were a child again. He was unbearably frustrated. The thought of insects and eyeless women brought gooseflesh to his arms and to the back of his neck.

—It's not true, Michael said.

—I'm only telling you what happened, Winston said. And he apologized.

. . .

The rest of the evening left only a few bland impressions on Michael. He went inside to have his picture taken. His father spoke to him about the ride home. His sister held him and kissed his cheek.

—What's the matter? his mother asked.

—He was talking to Winston Grant.

—Oho, said his mother. You know . . . Winston is a little strange . . .

And his uncle said:

—Don't pay attention to anything Winston tell you.

It was comforting to be reassured, but it was too late. Winston's story had been a hoax; that was certain. Michael was proud that he'd suspected it all along, but there was still some doubt. Why would anyone invent such an elaborate story? And if it *were* true? (He could almost see the house, could see the painting on the wall, could feel the beetles on his tongue.)

Winston had come to the wedding with his parents. He left with them before Michael could work up the nerve to ask him why he'd lied. One minute he was at his table in a corner of the hall; the next he was gone. And so, the second-to-last time Michael saw him, Winston was looking down at his own hands. It was remarkable how thin he was.

At midnight Michael left with his parents. The only people after them were revelers who would have to be cleared out, a few of the groom's people who stayed behind to clean the hall, and the disk jockey, who was carefully putting his records back in their sleeves. Outside, the night was cool, the sky starry, the moon a thin crescent.

As they drove, his parents argued about something insignificant. (It was the way they communicated. It wasn't clear they loved each other. It had never been obvious.) Twice during the long drive home Michael almost fell asleep. Twice he was woken by the imagined presence of someone beside him.

4.

It was almost gentle, the way his troubles began: alone in his room, warm in his bed. His window looked out onto the backyard, which was flooded with light from patio lanterns. The trees were black and spiky. Beyond the trees were office buildings, their windows lit up like white tiles. The physical world and everything in it was slightly sharper, and the sharpness reminded him of Mrs. Fernandez.

In his imagination, Mrs. Fernandez resembled his aunt Vio, whom he adored. As he drifted toward sleep, he could feel her hand on his forehead, a soothing weight. Then, suddenly, it became something else, something cold and heavy that called up a variety of images: young women, their faces unclear or hidden in shadow, their heads bent forward, their breasts swaying, a glimpse of erect nipples. He felt himself being touched, heard his name called, and it frightened him from sleep.

This happened again and again. He couldn't keep himself from thinking of the Soucouyant. Though he tried to think of pleasant things, his thoughts inevitably returned to the sharp world. He moved about in his bed, turning this way and that until his neck hurt and his body ached.

After four or five hours, it finally seemed as if his imagination would have mercy on him. He drifted into a light sleep, but this was worse than the physical torment it replaced: once past the soft dark of losing consciousness, he would find himself at Mrs. Fernandez's door, and then he was inside, aware of a presence, convinced he was being held by the ankles.

He was afraid to sleep; he was afraid to stay awake. He was afraid to lie still; he was afraid to move. And it wasn't just a fear of death or a fear of being bitten. It was as if the night itself loathed him. No amount of reasoning could undo the panic.

It was the dawn that finally put him to sleep.

The following nights were unbearable, and each was, in its way, a little worse, because Michael spent his days trying to convince himself that the coming night would be better, that he would sleep without thinking of Mrs. Fernandez.

By the third day, even Michael's father noticed his condition.

—What's wrong with you? he asked. You look awful. Let's take your temperature . . .

His temperature *was* a little high, so they fed him and sent him off to his room, to relax. (That was the problem when his father noticed things were wrong. He had one solution to everything: "Go and lie down." It wouldn't have occurred to him that you don't lie down to rest your soul.) And Michael did go off to sleep, and did sleep, and that night he didn't sleep at all. Instead, he kept vigil in his room, staring at the moon, aware of every sound in the house.

Still, this was the night his panic subsided.

It wasn't that Michael forgot Winston's story, nor that the idea of the Soucouyant no longer upset him. It was just that, for some reason, when he imagined Mrs. Fernandez's house or the beetles in her garden, he wasn't quite so frightened. He couldn't think of them with equanimity, but he had to concentrate to feel how terrifying they'd been.

By the fifth night, it was a struggle to recall the fear. He went over his impressions and dreams like turning ashes in a dying fire: only an occasional worm of light. He could no longer enter the house he'd imagined for Mrs. Fernandez. It grew vague and became a number of houses. It became the house in Petrolia where his turtles had died; the house in Sandy Hill in which his mother had thrown the dinner plates against the kitchen wall. And each house it became took him farther from the Soucouyant.

He did manage to keep up his resentment of Winston Grant, though. It had been unspeakably cruel to tell him such a story. Winston deserved whatever it was that was killing him. If they ever met again, Michael would pulverize him, even if Winston was a few years older.

.   .   .

It should all have ended there.

In the months that followed the wedding, a number of bewildering things intruded on Michael's imagination. His mother and father no longer spoke, no longer lived together. (His father had taken up with another woman, a white woman with a French accent.) His sister and her husband moved to Toronto, leaving Michael alone to comfort his mother, though he was too young to understand her suffering and he couldn't imagine what might comfort her. And, finally, his restlessness, the feeling that kept him apart from others, became almost unbearable. He couldn't sit still, and he hated to move.

Beneath all of this was something like dread, a sense that his fate had changed, a recurring memory of suffocation. Winston had broken Michael's faith in the unique world, and it upset him to feel the number of worlds that now existed at once.

And so, Michael and his mother lived in the house. Where once she had been his support, he tried to be hers. They even pretended to be equals, though once she stopped being maternal what was she but another member of an unpleasant world? For a while, he listened to her stories of his father's endless cruelties. (It was as Michael had always suspected: his father was incapable of love.) But it was pity that made him attentive, and when that was exhausted he stopped listening, or listened only to what interested him.

—You know, she said one night as they ate together at the big table, Mrs. Grant's boy died last week.

—Who? Michael asked.

—Winston, the boy at Mimi's wedding . . . Weren't you two friends?

Michael looked up from his plate.

—Weren't you friends?

Michael suddenly experienced the earth in spring: the fields black, the sky watery blue, broken bottles by the roadside . . .

—How did he die?

—Something in the blood, I think. Poor Wilma is so upset. Winston was their only child, you know . . .

Which was all she could manage before she started to cry. (He was lucky, he thought, that his mother had gotten that far. Lately, she was as likely to break down at a commercial for cat food as she was at bad news.) It made him long for the days when his family had been close. Even Mimi's wedding, a mere six months ago, now seemed like brighter days (though it had been the beginning of the end).

Three nights later, Michael dreamt of Winston:

He had decided to visit Winston. Mrs. Fernandez's house was easily recognized: moss had overrun the place. Its windows, though, were unobscured, and Michael could see into the living room: dull furniture; bottles of darkly colored something left about the room. The other houses on the street were identically red-bricked, with plumes of smoke rising from their chimneys. When he knocks at her door, Mrs. Fernandez answers immediately. "Winston?" she says. "So long he ain' workin' here." And she closes the door. He's about to leave when the woman next door calls him over. She goes on and on about the sky and the building before mentioning her problem with beetles: they've overrun her garden. She and Michael go to the back of her house. Everything is white: the lawn, the fence, the dirt, the sky above them. In Mrs. Fernandez's backyard, the ground is dark and Mrs. Fernandez is on her knees, burying bottles in the ground. In a window on the second floor, Winston stands immobile, his hands up to protect himself. Michael looks away, and when he looks back Winston is still immobile, but his arms have moved. It's like watching still photographs of a bird flying into a window: Winston's face is contorted, his mouth open, his eyes closed. He looks ecstatic . . .

And then, as dreams will, it became something else, from another part of his subconscious.

For all intents and purposes, this was the last time he saw Winston Grant.

It wasn't the last time he saw Mrs. Fernandez.

He went looking for the Soucouyant.

Kuala Lumpur

The house was filled with mourners.

One of them stood up and called for quiet:

—I would just like to say a few words about Doctor Williams. In my opinion, he was the very best of men. One would have to search far and wide to find his equal, to find someone as kind, generous, and honest as the Doctor. I would not presume to judge this man, this paragon of virtue, but I, like so many of you here today, must despair of finding one so good. I say, with the great poets, we will not soon see his like again. I myself remember when I first met the Doctor. It was not a happy occasion for me. I had a boil on my bottom, because my pants had chafed and it was torture for me to sit down . . . It was not the most auspicious of introductions, as I was sensitive about my injury, but the Doctor put me at ease, and before I knew what happened, he lanced the offending thing, put a bandage on for me, and sent me on my way with the smile we have all come to know and love. After that, I did not hesitate to visit him for my problems, and not once, no matter how private the matter, did the Doctor turn me away . . . I would like all of you to join me now in a toast to his memory: To the Doctor, and may God look after him as he looked after us!

And they all stood up and drank to his father's memory.

For Michael, this wake was more upsetting than his father's death had been. His father's death had come after a painful struggle, peacefully. There had been no time to say this or that, and very little contact between them. (The day before he died, he tried to squeeze Michael's hand, but Michael had pulled his hand away immediately.)

Now, three days later, he was in a living room he barely recognized, with people he had met once or twice, if at all, and a handful of relatives.

A young woman in a black dress put her hand on his shoulder. Her hair was thick and black as a stage wig, and on her head she had what looked like a white lace doily.

—Poor boy, she said. You'll have to be strong now. For your dear mother . . .

She couldn't have been much older than he was, but she spoke maternally.

—He's so strong for his age, she said.

And that's how it had been all day. The mourners evidently felt they owed him the benefit of their wisdom, but when it came right down to it, they had none to offer.

Mr. Taylor, the man who'd given the toast to his father's memory, approached and said:

—How're you, young fellow?

—Fine, Michael answered.

—He was a damned good man, the Doctor . . .

Mr. Taylor smelled of alcohol and, beneath that, mothballs.

—Your father brought my own two into the world, he said. Wouldn't have anyone else do it. My wife, that's her, she felt the same way about it. Wouldn't have anyone else do it. The way these doctors are today, you don't find a good one too soon, that's for sure . . . Did you like my speech?

—Yes, Michael politely said.

—Two days to write it, said Mr. Taylor. Just to show how much we loved the Doctor.

He put his hand on Michael's shoulder, and then he moved on.

Michael's mother was in the kitchen with his aunt Edna. It was they who had made the peas and rice, the stewed chicken, and the fish cakes. They had also made the ginger ale, and all the little sweets left on white plates, on tables and counters around the house. The two of them had been in the kitchen for days, for weeks it seemed. And before that, they had moved the furniture around, turned the paintings to face the wall, and hung crepe over all the mirrors.

His mother was in a dowdy black dress, her face made up; cheeks rouged, eyelashes blackened, and she smelled of the Chanel they had given her for Christmas years ago.

One of the guests said:

—I've never had a better peas and rice . . .

—Thank you, Russell, his mother said.

She sounded tired.

His uncle Horace, who sat with two men Michael had never met, called him over. He put his arm around Michael's waist.

—Michael, this is Fred Hosein, and this is Melvin Fernandez. They were your father's friends back home.

—He looks just like Sonny, said Mr. Fernandez.

—You find?

Horace held him loosely. The men went on talking about Trinidad.

As soon as it was polite, Michael moved away from them. He made for the kitchen, but before he could get there a woman pulled him to her breast and held him. She smelled of rose water and baby powder. She held on to him until he thought he would suffocate, but no, she let him go, held him again, then let him go for good: all without a word.

—Michael! Come give your mother a hand, his aunt Edna called.

But there was nothing for him to do, really. The latest course was ready, but as with the drink, people preferred to help themselves. (The mourners had finished the ginger beer, the coffee, the innocuous things. They were now on to stronger smack.)

—What do you want me to do? Michael asked.

But nobody was listening. His mother and his aunt were bickering about the salt in the stewed chicken.

—Don't put too much, you'll ruin it, his mother said.

As Michael retreated from the kitchen, a certain Mr. Andrew took hold of his arm. He introduced Michael to Mrs. Andrew. Mrs. Andrew was short, thin, and gray-haired. She was dressed in black and, despite the heat, she still wore her black pillbox hat.

—This is the Doctor's son, said Mr. Andrew.

—He looks so much like the Doctor, said Mrs. Andrew.

The sound of people chatting, of glasses clinking, of subdued laughter: it was annoying.

—Lovely funeral, said Mrs. Andrew.

Mr. Andrew said:

—The Doctor would have liked it.

Michael smiled politely, but it was impossible for him to imagine his father pleased with *any* funeral, much less his own. (Still, he doesn't have to make conversation, Michael thought, and the thought consoled him.)

—You know, said Mr. Andrew, not to change the conversation, but do you watch television?

—Yes.

—Of course . . . so I wonder if you saw . . . what was the name? . . . The one about funerals?

He turned to Mrs. Andrew.

—"The Hour of Our Death," she said.

—That's it: "The Hour of Our Death." Did you see it?

—No, said Michael.

Mr. Andrew said:

—It was remarkable. Where was it? Kuala Lumpur? It said the people in Kuala Lumpur, they put the son to death when the father dies . . . Isn't that something? If the son looks too much like the father, they put him to death . . .

The Andrews stared at Michael as if there were a correct response to this.

—I look like my mother, Michael said.

Mr. Andrew said:

—No, no . . . I didn't mean . . .

Mrs. Andrew put her hand on Michael's arm.

—He didn't mean . . .

—It's all right, said Michael.

But he moved away from them.

There were people everywhere. Downstairs, a young couple had discovered his bedroom. They were sitting on his bed.

—I hope we're not in the way, said the woman.

—Your father was a good man, said the man.

They went on talking to each other.

It really was a peculiar wake, but he wasn't sure his own feelings weren't behind its quirks. It was lacking solemnity, but he himself didn't feel solemn. (There were too many people. It was difficult to feel anything at all.) There should have been more sorrow or more distress. Instead, everyone spoke of The Doctor, and they held on to him. (It was like being wrapped in wet cotton.) And then, periodically, like a wave of nausea, his own grief rose and it was all he could do to keep from crying.

He went from room to room looking for quiet. There were people in all of them: in the kitchen, in all

three bathrooms, in the living room, in all five bedrooms, in the dining room, in the bar, in the family
room . . . no sanctuary.

Worse, as time went on their voices were less hushed;
their laughter not quite restrained.

—Come hear this . . .

—Remember Admiral Nelson?

—Is there a little more sorrel?

—I'm so sorry, Mrs. Williams. He was a good man . . .

And then Mr. Taylor, who'd been drinking since his first
eulogy, called for quiet. He didn't get it, though his wife
managed to shush a few of the people around him.

—I want to say a few words about Doctor Williams,
said Mr. Taylor. The Doctor was a good man. He
was . . . generous, and good, and kind, and he never
looked down on people who didn't have money . . . I remember the first time I saw the Doctor. It was a happy
occasion . . . No, it wasn't happy. I had a boil, and the
Doctor had to lance it, but the Doctor didn't hesitate.
After that, I didn't hesitate to bring up private matters,
because I knew the Doctor wouldn't mind. That was
the kind of man he was . . .

Though very few people were listening to him, Mr.
Taylor struggled manfully to remember the rest of his
speech. His wife encouraged him. Nothing more would
come, though.

—The Doctor! he said at last.

And the people nearest him drank politely from
their glasses.

There *were* a few who seemed genuinely upset by

his father's death. Even now, hours after the burial, they wiped the tears from their eyes. Were they upset by his father's death, by death itself, or was there something else?

Having listened to Mr. Taylor's second, sad eulogy, Michael again made his way through the crowd. (It had grown.) He was on his way downstairs when Father Albert pulled him aside.

—Michael? How're you holding up?

—I'm fine.

—Don't be afraid to let it out, Michael. I know sometimes we men tend to keep things in, but it's good to let things out . . .

—Thank you, Father.

—Women are better with their emotions. No doubt about it . . . Just last month I was at a funeral in Wakefield. Not a dry eye in the house, *except* for the son. You'd think he didn't care peanuts. And then, next thing you know, schizophrenia. He's looking, speaking, and acting like his father. You couldn't have told them apart. Lost himself entirely. Isn't that something?

—Yes, said Michael.

—So you just let it out.

—Thank you, Father.

In his bedroom, the couple were intimate: he now had his hand politely placed on her knee; she had hers on his shoulder. They sat facing each other, each with one foot on the floor, their bodies slightly reclined on his bed.

—I hope we're not in the way, the woman said.

Neither of them moved.

—No, said Michael.

It was he who was in the way, though all he wanted was to lie in his own bed with the lights out.

—Your father was a good man, the man said.

What was he supposed to say to that? His feelings for his father would not fit under the word "good." "Good" was no help at all. His father had been loving, kind, cruel, mean, headstrong, unloving, playful, gentle, and on until all the adjectives were exhausted. He had loved his father, he supposed, though here, as ever, the word "love" was puny. It wasn't love he felt for his father, but it was love also.

By the time he had made his way back upstairs, the mourners had become even more animated. (There were more of them.) There was some confusion. Someone was arguing about Jamaican cooking. Someone else excitedly spoke of a television program on the life of mollusks. And every time Michael passed a clump of people, someone would reach out for him.

—Your father . . . , they'd say.

Or:

—He loved you . . .

Or:

—You look so much like him . . .

And someone said:

—There was a something on *Nature* last week about Kuala Lumpur . . .

And it reminded Michael of eucalyptus trees.

. . .

Who were these people, anyway? He was beginning to wonder if it was such a good thing that so many people's lives had been salved by his father's art.

An older woman pulled his arm as he passed.

—You know, she said, your father loved you. He told me so himself, but . . . I don't know how to say this . . . maybe he was a little worried about you too. And he wasn't exactly sure what you were doing with your life. I mean, here you are eighteen . . . Are you eighteen? Seventeen? Anyway, you need direction in life, and he wasn't really sure what direction you were taking . . . He wanted to see direction, that's all . . . I'd call that a good father, wouldn't you? To love you like that when you were breaking his heart a little, even though you didn't mean to . . . but you were a little bit of a disappointment, you know . . . not a disappointment, exactly, just a sliver of a disappointment . . . but that goes to show how much he loved you, doesn't it? Even though you were a disappointment . . .

Then she let go of him and turned away as if she hadn't spoken to him at all.

There were more people crying now. Two or three of them were in real distress. One stood sobbing in a corner of the living room. There was a respectful distance between him and those nearby.

And then it was as if his family disappeared. He couldn't find them in the crush of strangers. But no, there they were, when he actually looked for them: his mother and his aunt in the kitchen, his sister and her husband in the dining room, the rest of them dispersed throughout, drinking.

Again, he ventured downstairs. The man and woman were still in his bedroom. Their relationship had progressed. His hand was frankly near her breast. It was there in a friendly way, but it had an intent of some sort. Her hand was casually open on his lap. Their faces were inches apart.

He was about to say something when the woman looked up.

—Oh, she said. I hope we're not in the way . . .

Michael stood before them, watching their hands. He knew their hands.

—Your father was a good man, the man said.

His room was no longer his to use. (He didn't want to face those two again.) That left only four rooms to which he could retire for privacy. There was the bathroom downstairs: newly wainscoted, it smelled of pine. There was the bathroom upstairs: tiled not two months ago, it smelled of caulking. There was the bathroom adjoining his parents' bedroom: it was too small. Finally, there was the furnace room. From each bathroom he would have to chase mourners or, worse, mourners engaged in the legitimate use of the accommodations. In any case, he didn't want to spend the day chasing people from bathrooms.

That left the furnace room. It was a clean chamber at the other end of the basement. It was well lit and smelled only a little of oil, and it was unlikely anyone would choose to do their mourning there. It was, suddenly, a haven.

He made his way through the dark suits and dresses as if he were penetrating a thick curtain, feeling for the part.

—Excuse me, young fellow, said Mr. So and So.

—Michael? said Father Albert. How're you holding up?

—I'm so sorry, said an older woman with white hair. She held on to him.

—Are you Michael? said an older man.

He held on to him.

The place was now unbearably loud. It smelled of powders, colognes, sweat, and alcohol. It was a relief to reach the furnace room, and then, as he should have guessed, the furnace room was occupied. There were three people inside: his uncle Roger, a stranger in a blue suit, and a woman in a blue dress wearing a floppy blue hat with a wide white band.

—Just close the door there for me, will you, Michael?

—Is this Michael? the woman asked.

She hugged him.

—We knew your father, said the man.

He touched Michael's shoulder.

—He was a good man.

They stared at him, as though admiring his clothes, and tried to engage him in conversation.

Bitterly disappointed, Michael made his way back through the crowd. As he did, he happened to see the clock behind the bar. Six o'clock! Four hours had passed since his father had been put in the ground. Time was an accordion. Certain things felt as if they'd gone on forever (a speech, a discussion), while others had breezed by (a speech, an encounter). The wake was like a fever, like lying in bed, the smell of a blanket like a horse's mane, the hours short, the minutes eternal.

Upstairs, the noise of conversation fought with the noise of grief. The man in the corner was even more distraught. He beat his chest and cried out. It was grotesque, but his grief was contagious. Hundreds of mourners were in tears. Now, when they held Michael they inadvertently dug their nails into his biceps or shook him or forced his head onto their breasts and held it there, his nose crushed on their sternums.

Once again, Mr. Taylor called for silence. He tried to stand up on a chair, failed, tried again, one hand on his wife's head for support. Mrs. Taylor was stoic under pressure. Mr. Taylor held up his hands.

—Shhh . . . , he said. Shhhh . . .

It would have been difficult to hear him, even if one were paying close attention. No one was.

—The Doctor, he said. The Doctor . . . boils and all . . . stand still, dammit! . . . a paragon of injury . . . you stand there naked while he's sticking your boils . . . nothing personal . . . you better believe it . . . he was a good man . . . stand still!

And then he was helped down from the chair, or pulled down, by several men who thought he might hurt himself if he fell. Mr. Taylor was insulted by the idea. He attacked his wife.

—You bitch! he said.

But his insults were as slurred as his eulogy had been. They were lost in the din. And when he saw that most of the people around him were openly weeping, Mr. Taylor began to weep as well.

A woman in a navy-blue dress pulled back the wire-mesh curtain on the fireplace. She sprinkled ashes on her forehead. And then, the rest of them began to do the same. They took handfuls of ashes. They opened their shirts and dresses to find expanses of skin to cover. They ripped their clothes. A cloud of ashes rose over the living room.

Someone dug their nails into Michael's elbow. (It was as if he'd cut himself on a broken bottle.)

—Spitting image, she said.

Father Albert held him by the collar.

—Let it out, he said.

But he couldn't. The ground shook from the mourners who stamped their feet as they covered themselves with ashes and called out his father's name. Michael could barely make his way through the crowd. The basement was no longer accessible, but the confusion and grief had certainly found their way downstairs. The noise that came from below was just as frightening as that from the main floor.

—In Male . . .

—In Kuala Lumpur . . .

—In Kuala Lumpur?

. . .

Just what was the point of a wake, anyway? To revel in the memory of the dead? To share a common sorrow? Canadians didn't do that kind of thing, did they? He himself couldn't revel and he felt no sorrow. He felt nothing definite: sadness, longing, fear, resentment . . . there was even a small place where he was relieved by his father's death. He couldn't cry, while these people, many of whom knew his father only as The Doctor, these were the people who wept and covered themselves with ashes. Their tears were real; their cries were convincing, while all he could manage was to wander about, pushing his way through the mourners like an usher. He deserved whatever they had planned for him.

Briefly, he caught sight of his mother. Her face was pale, her hair disheveled, her clothes rumpled. Her eye shadow had run and her makeup had noticeably pebbled. She was no more than two yards away, but there were too many people between them. She was eclipsed by a tall man with ashes on his forehead.

An old man pinched Michael's cheek. A woman held him from behind.

—It's been so long, she said. Don't you recognize me?

—No, Michael said.

He couldn't even see her. She held on, squeezing the wind out of him.

—Where's Michael? someone shouted.

And from somewhere else came the sound of breaking glass.

The mourners still took great handfuls of ash from

the fireplace. (I should have cleaned the fireplace when he asked me, Michael thought.) A woman tore the front of her own dress and then ripped the arm from the jacket of the man beside her. He in turn pulled his white shirt open with such force the buttons hit the wall like hail on shutters. (I should have cleaned the ashes in February or March, thought Michael.) Three women stood by the stairs to the basement. They had torn their dresses down to their petticoats. They were covered in ashes, and they sang:

—Save me, O God; for the waters are come in unto my soul . . .

As if there weren't enough noise in the house.

And the noise had become something like a long groan of anguish. Michael finally broke free of the woman holding him.

—The boy doesn't remember his mother's best friend! What kind of son is that?

More than anything else in the world, Michael needed to get outside. The wake had degenerated into something ecstatic and unhealthy. There were people shouting, crying, pulling their clothes from their bodies, breaking dishes against the wall, calling out his father's name. They moved aside at his approach, thousands of them, pushing him toward the living room, toward the fireplace. (It was like drowning, with someone there to push you down or pull you under.)

And Michael began to struggle. He saw himself in the third person, fighting their will. He noticed peculiar details as he resisted: the rouge on a man's face, a false eyelash that hung down like a spider, a yellow shirt, a small turquoise ring, gold cuff links, a handprint in ashes on the forehead of a young woman. He struggled, but on toward the fireplace he went. They wanted him. They wanted to touch him, to say: "Cry, it's all right. We care for you. He was a good man. You look just like him." And then they were going to burn him. It was all clear to him, in the fever of grief. He sank to his hands and knees and crawled through the wilderness of legs and feet, toward the nearest wall.

—Where's Michael? someone shouted.

—Excuse me, Michael said, as he snuck through their legs. I've lost my contact lenses.

He didn't wear contact lenses, but the mourners moved aside just the same. It took him five minutes to reach a wall, and when he did he held to it.

—Michael! his mother called.

And then her voice was lost in the noise. What did she want? It didn't matter. He kept moving.

They looked down at him, but all they could see clearly was the back of his suit, his neck bent forward, his knuckles and fingers in the deep carpet. He was anonymous, but his progress through the crowd was slow.

And then he could see the door, but the foyer was empty. Should he remain where he was, hidden by the legs of a few mourners, or should he make a break for the door? If he stayed where he was, the mourners would find him or trample him underfoot. If he made for the door, they would see him in the foyer. It was ten yards to the door, plenty of room to tackle him if he were seen.

—Michael? someone said softly.

And touched his shoulder. So the decision was made for him. He ran for the door. He made it across the foyer and, pulling frantically, twisted the large, brass doorknob this way and that.

—Michael?

Was the last thing he heard.

Outside, the sun was on its way down. It was still light, but the earth smelled of weeds and the close of day. The river ran softly by. The houses on the other shore were small and bright.

It was strange to go from such commotion to such peace. Standing there beside the water, looking across at the other shore, he felt the weight of silence. There was no one else in the world. There was Michael, and there was earth, sky, trees, and water.

Gradually, the stillness of the world settled on him.

And then, for a moment, he distinctly felt his father's hand in his. He looked up at his father's face as they crossed a street in Petrolia, Ontario . . .

He remembered the warmth of his father's hand.

Everything else was hidden in a confusion of emotions . . .

A confusion, a welter, a tangle, a tumult . . .

Metaphysics of Morals

In the morning, Irene discovered there was no bread. Without bread, they couldn't really have breakfast. So, at eight o'clock, she pulled the covers from him and said something about the corner store.

Michael got up, but he was still sleepy. He put on his tanned, weather-mauled shoes, then took them off so he could put his socks on first. If he'd had to defend a meager supply of winter grain from a band of marauders, well, perhaps *then* he might have skipped the socks. With his leather shoes snugly tied to his feet, armed with an ax, he would have defended his home . . . Of course, in that situation going without socks would have been no more than self-preservation; the same as putting on socks was now. The enemy routed were like socks remembered, or so he imagined as he walked out of the house, coat unbuttoned, shoestrings untied, socks drooping.

Above him, the sky was clear and blue. Snow had

fallen and done its worst: the earth would be white for days . . .

And then, for no reason at all, Michael felt the presence of God. It was very nearly palpable, as though the trees might catch fire, or his soul disperse in all directions . . .

It was interesting: Irene had woken him, saying:

—We're out of bread.

And now here he was: unmoored, out for bread in the hands of God. (It was thoughts like these that made you *want* to shop.)

On Bank Street a woman brushed by him. She was taller than he. Her red winter coat hung like a funnel from her shoulders. He saw the soft curve of a pink cheek, the side of a chin, and what might have been a touch of down on her upper lip. What attracted him, however, was the way she held her black leather gloves: in one hand, loosely, as though they were for riding.

As she walked away, one of the gloves fell unnoticed to the pavement. Before he could stop himself, Michael bent down, picked it up, and quickened his pace. He had every intention of returning it. A few steps and he would be there by her mysterious and infundibulously sensual side . . . Instead, he turned a corner and walked away from her, casually, making no effort to hide the glove, looking, in fact, as though he had no idea to whom the glove belonged.

This maneuver, this turning away, was quite interesting: in order to turn casually away (with the woman's glove), Michael needed a reason. It wouldn't do to simply run (with the woman's glove). That would have attracted attention to his flight, as would a hasty detour. It all had to look natural, even justified. So, in the few seconds it took to decide (to keep the woman's glove), Michael's mind had to provide him with a solid reason for turning away. And the reason was this: Carlo's Corner Store. He turned off Bank Street and onto MacLaren to buy his bread at Carlo's. This is what he would have answered had someone asked where he was going with the glove: "I'm going to Carlo's." It didn't matter, just then, that Carlo's was seedy, smelled of stale French tobacco, and stocked bread that was unfailingly green. In fact, this was some-how to the store's credit. For, having kept moldy bread in the past, it was sure to have fresh bread now. In the past, he and Irene had bought mouse-eaten bread, rot-ten oysters, rancid soup, and tainted salmon from Carlo. Now, however, and Michael *really* felt this, it was his turn to find good bread. Thus was he justified in turning down this street (MacLaren), away from the reliable Herb and Spice (which was on Bank). If there was good bread at Carlo's, it was his turn to get it.

He felt a little selfish, though, embarrassed even. There had been no reason to take the glove. He didn't really want it. He'd simply acted on impulse. There was still time to return it, but he didn't want to do that either. It was a moral quandary. He turned and looked back toward Bank Street, but the woman was gone.

Casually, he brought the glove to his nose and inhaled its perfume. It smelled faintly of leather, and of something human. It was exactly as he imagined it would be: soft to the touch, with a lining of beige synthetic fur. And then, all of a sudden, the whole business was banal and silly. He felt ridiculous with a stranger's glove at his nose. He let it fall to the street. It hit the sidewalk beside the wheel of a parked car.

The door to Carlo's Corner Store jangled as it opened, creaked, and then closed behind him. Carlo was behind the counter, and because Carlo was older and sensitive to the cold, the little store was hot as a steam room.

—Keep the door closed, Carlo said.

His face was round, white, and doughy, with a strap of gray hair beneath his chin. His eyes, or what could be seen of them under their heavy pink lids, were watery blue. And, as he did every day, Carlo calmly presided over his warm and narrow store. To one side were the dry goods, on largely empty shelves; to the other were canned things. Down the center was a two-sided shelf with everything else Carlo had to offer, including bread. The place stank of stale tobacco.

As Michael reached for the bread, Carlo said:

—Don't feel the bread. It's fresh.

Ignoring him, Michael picked up one of the loaves.

—Why touch the bread? You don't trust me?

The bread wasn't anywhere near "fresh." It was green with mold, and its white, plastic ring indicated it was a month past due.

—Buy it, you'll see it's fresh, Carlo said.

Warring instincts fought for Michael's soul. He

wanted to walk out of the store, but he was held there by the memory of the woman's glove. He deserved Carlo's, no doubt, but how would he explain all this to Irene? ("I took a woman's glove, so I felt the need to punish myself with Carlo's bread.") Also, he felt he couldn't leave without buying *something*. It wouldn't look right. (Was this how Carlo made his money, through moral ambivalence?) And then, right beside the bread, he saw his salvation: a bag of reasonably fresh pitas.

—Why don't you take the bread too, Carlo said. It's fresh.

Could it be that Carlo didn't know his bread was moldy? Michael tried to look the old man in the eye, but Carlo wasn't looking at him. He was staring at the pitas on the counter.

—Dollar fifty, he said.

And slowly, he put his pudgy hand on the bag of pitas and pulled them toward him. With the other hand, its thick fingers, he took a small paper bag from beneath the counter. It was difficult for him to do these things. He was breathing heavily as he opened the bag and pushed the pitas in. That was that. He turned away from Michael, took up the cigarette he had beside him on a small, white plate, and inhaled.

—Thank you, Michael said.

Outside, the morning air was now bracing. Michael was fully awake, and the sun was higher above the clouds. Or so it appeared to him. The woman's glove was still on the ground, but he looked away from it (a mite conspicuously, drawing attention to himself perhaps? No, there was no one about) and walked on.

As he crossed Bank, he reflected on what he'd done. He had no idea why he'd taken the damned glove. Perhaps it had been sheer ill will, a feeling that had slithered from his tripes and overtaken him, a smidgen of evil that had surfaced without being summoned and dissipated without being savored. Then again . . . what was so evil about stealing a glove? It hadn't even been a proper theft: an impulse, nothing more, a will-o'-the-wisp that had clouded his civic-mindedness. No, sir . . . it was flattery to call it evil. Evil, as he conceived it, was poking out a baby's eye with a stick, or forcing a woman in her eighties to perform oral sex, or sticking knives into a corpse . . . Although . . . looked at objectively, as he crossed Lyon behind a Volkswagen that fishtailed by, that is, from the vantage of God, were these acts really evil? After all, the child would be one-eyed, but more or less healthy; the eighty-year-old would not die from the indignity; and as to the corpse, it would neither feel nor suffer anything at all. And yet . . . it took all of his concentration to think of these things without revulsion, without imagining the bristle on the old woman's ear or the spittle on the baby's chin. And so he discovered that it was not the pain others suffered that prevented him from doing them harm. It was his own: it was the pain he imagined he would feel were he to commit any of these indignities. That's what kept him in line. (And, as he crossed Percy Street, he felt elated by his own acumen.) It thus followed that he was only as "good" as his imagination. Were he suddenly unable to imagine pain, he would poke out eyes at will. With that thought, Michael believed he had solved the mystery of morality. He was onto something important. As he put his hand on the door to his house, the light of reason descended. In that instant it was as though he were a bearer of wisdom . . .

—Michael? Irene called.

—Uhmmm?

—Just checking. Did you get the bread?

Michael shut the door behind him, carefully.

—I thought I'd get something different, he said.

—What?

—Thought I'd try something different. Pita.

Irene was in the kitchen. She came out to look at him.

—Pita?

—Sure. Why not?

—With bacon and eggs?

—Sure. It'll be Middle Eastern. You know . . . it wouldn't hurt to live like the Arabs once in a while.

She couldn't tell if he was joking.

—Arabs don't eat bacon, she said.

—That's not the point. I just thought it would be good to try and imagine what the world's like over there, with all the violence and everything, but if you want me to go back and get good old Wonder bread . . .

There wasn't much you could say to that, so Irene said:

—No, no . . . It's all right, I guess . . .

And returned to the kitchen where the bacon was smoking in the frying pan.

Their breakfast was unsatisfying. The pita wasn't right: it was difficult to toast. You couldn't butter it. It simply didn't belong on a plate with bacon and eggs. Every so often, Irene said:

—Well, it's not so bad . . .

And he answered:

—No, you could really get used to it . . .

But they both knew they'd seen the last of pita for breakfast.

Afterward, once the dishes had been washed and set to dry, the two of them returned to bed. It was Saturday morning. There was nothing urgent to buy, sell, perform, or destroy. The hours lay before them like a Persian rug on which the name of Allah is a recurrent Mediterranean blue. They snuggled up to keep warm and pulled their favorite blanket up to their chins. Irene turned on the radio and listened to the classics while Michael drifted back to sleep.

Thoughts of comfort and feelings of love led him to the door of a room, and then, from somewhere far away, the Mormon Tabernacle choir sang "Hark the Herald Angels Sing," and Michael returned to his childhood.

· II ·

Despair

FIVE STORIES OF OTTAWA

1.

There was a man named Martin Bjornson who lived, precisely, at 128 MacLaren. He lived with his mother (whom he knew as Mrs. Bjornson) and a fifty-year-old parakeet named Knut. The parakeet had learned to cough and spit like a tubercular old man, sounding much as Martin's father Frederic had sounded, but it was otherwise unremarkable.

One night, while the Bjornsons were at home playing a game of two-handed whist, Knut coughed, spit up, and then said, quite distinctly it seemed to Martin, "Jesus, Maria, my corns are killing me." These were Knut's first and last words. After pronouncing them, he keeled over and died. The Bjornsons were as surprised by Knut's unexpected revelation as they were by the sudden death that followed it. It took them quite some time to finish their game of whist (won by Mrs. Bjornson with a flourish of trump). When they had finished, and when he discovered that his mother was *not* named Maria, Martin said:

—Did you understand what Knut meant, Mother?

—Did Knut speak? asked Mrs. Bjornson.

—Yes, he did, said Martin.

And he resolved to get to the bottom of the matter.

The day after Knut's demise, Martin began to wander the streets of the city repeating aloud the parakeet's final words—"Jesus, Maria, my corns are killing me"—in the hope that someone who recognized the phrase would unveil its mystery to him. The results were unpromising at first. After a week of wandering, the only people who had spoken to him were a panhandler named Morris and a dental assistant named Antoinette Lachapelle. Finally, Martin was heard by a pharmacist named Mario Prater who understood him to be saying "Jeez, Mario, my corns are hurting me." Mr. Prater, suppressing his disdain at such a blunt request for help, answered that adhesive pads were available for any foot. What he said was:

—You know, foot pads could help you there.

Which Martin mistook for a reference to a "Mr. Paz."

—Paz? Martin asked.

—Yes, answered Mr. Prater.

Martin thanked the pharmacist by pressing six or seven quarters into the palm of his hand and mentioning that, given enough notice, he and his mother would be pleased to have him dine with them.

—Smorgasbord! Martin said as he walked away.

Now, despite the cheerfully given invitation, this encounter was an unhappy one for the pharmacist, and it proved to be a tragic one for the Bjornsons. It was unhappy for the pharmacist because he felt ambivalent about being seen to take spare change from a passerby. (He let the coins drop into his pocket, straightened his bow tie, and whistled as he walked away.) It was an unlucky exchange for Martin because, although his mother did not know any "Paz," she did know a Mr. Prinz. (This particular *Prinz* had seduced her before her marriage to Mr. Bjornson, when she had been a girl in Carleton Place.) And when her son told her that Mr. Paz had had something to do with "Maria's corns," she understood him to say that Mr. Prinz had had something to do with them. Her heart began to palpitate. She had trouble breathing, and then she gave up the ghost. (She had kept her first name from Martin precisely because she feared he might one day discover her connection to Mr. *Prinz*, his biological father.)

Mrs. Bjornson's death left Martin without father, mother, or family pet. In the face of such loss, it took real determination to carry on his search for the meaning of Knut's last words. But, after burying his mother in the clay behind their home, Martin carried on.

Mr. Paz, the only F. Paz in Ottawa, lived in the West End, behind the Merivale Shopping Centre. He was a blessèd man, devout and careful. He remembered all of his sins as though he had just committed them, and he suffered for them. So, when he saw Martin coming up his driveway, he thought he recognized the son of the only woman with whom he had committed fornication, a sin that was just then on his mind, and he rushed out to face him.

—I know what you're going to say, said Mr. Paz, and I'm not completely innocent, but your mother, you know, your mother wasn't always . . . honest . . .

—What do you mean?

—She was a good woman, but she was just a little bit of a liar, said Mr. Paz humbly.

—Make that clear, Martin said.

—I'm afraid she told me she wasn't married when we met. And she mentioned that she had a parrot that could recite Leviticus backward and forward . . .

—I didn't even know Knut could speak, said Martin.

—Knut? asked Mr. Paz. Was that the parrot? It couldn't say a word. She said that to seduce me, don't you know . . .

Martin struck Mr. Paz with his fist and left him lying on the ground. Mr. Paz lay on the green grass with his arms out, like a man crucified. Soon Mr. Paz's body rose from the lawn; his body rose. It ascended. It floated above the houses in Merivale. It sailed over the thousands of freshly tarred roofs. It passed by tall buildings and from the ground it appeared to be a cross or a starfish, and then a speck in the sunlight.

Martin returned to his home angry and discouraged. He did not know that Mr. Paz was dead and that he had been the cause of his death. That night he kept his mother company, sitting by her grave. It was a summer evening and there was a slight, warm wind. The wind reminded Martin of silence, and the silence reminded him of Mrs. Bjornson. And he thought of the mysterious ways by which death enters the world.

2.

At precisely 128 Beausoleil, there lived a Russian translator named Leo Chung. He lived alone in a small apartment on the 11th floor. He had few possessions, and what furniture there was had been passed over by the thieves who regularly entered and stole from the apartments in the building. It was well known that 128 was not a good address.

On a Saturday, Mr. Chung was laundering his shirt and tie in the building's basement laundry. He could hear people congregating in the meeting room beside him, and when it grew particularly noisy he looked in.

In the meeting room, tenants from all over the building sat in folding chairs before a large block of clear ice that stood beside a desk at the far end of the room. The building's superintendent stood on the desk. In the ice was the body of a certain Alfred Paradis, Mr. Chung's neighbor on the 11th floor. Mr. Paradis's face was blue as powdered bleach. The superintendent was addressing the crowd.

— . . . Once again, he said, I'd like to thank you men for your good work. We'll never know, like Mrs. Korzinski said the other day, *why* Paradis here stole our things, but by golly we got him . . . As I was saying to myself the other day, here's a man with so much stolen furniture in his place you couldn't get anywhere without climbing . . .

—Are you going to bury him? Mr. Chung asked from his side of the room.

—He doesn't deserve it! someone shouted.

—C'était un monstre, said the widow Paradis.

—He'd be expensive to put under, said the super-intendent.

—I'll pay, Mr. Chung said.

There was an anti-Oriental silence.

—Well, said Mrs. Paradis, si c'est lui qui va payer I don't care . . . (Mrs. Paradis thought: He was good to the kids. But, though the kids had climbed happily over the side tables, armchairs, and love seats to get at the bathroom, she couldn't count the number of times she had almost lost it on the furniture.)

—We bury him, then, said the superintendent.

And he rapped on the block of ice with his gavel.

Almost two weeks later, Mr. Chung lay in bed, asleep. He was woken by the sound of dry coughing. When he turned on his bedside lamp, he found he was almost face-to-face with Alfred Paradis, who sat in the chair beside his bed, and whose face was as baby blue as the last time Mr. Chung had seen it.

—Did I wake you? Mr. Paradis asked.

—Yes, said Mr. Chung.

—No problem. I just wanted to thank you. Hard to thank a man while he's asleep . . .

—Of course . . .

—It was a good thing you did, getting me a real burial.

Mr. Paradis scratched himself.

—I'll tell you, said Mr. Paradis, death doesn't cure psoriasis. I still scratch like a dog . . .

—Is there anything else? Mr. Chung asked.

—Yes, said Mr. Paradis. I give you three wishes, you know.

—Fine, said Mr. Chung. I'll think about it.

—Take your time . . .

Throughout the night, Mr. Paradis did indeed scratch like a dog. It sounded like someone shaking a bag full of leaves, and it kept Mr. Chung on the edge of sleep for hours. In the morning, Mr. Paradis sat at Mr. Chung's kitchen table blinking vigorously.

—You drink coffee? he asked.

—Yes, said Mr. Chung.

—Let me have some. It's not instant, is it? Darned little brown things that melt in water. How do you know that's coffee? Could be cockroach dung for all you know . . . So, do you have any wishes?

—I don't want anything, said Mr. Chung.

—Go on, said Mr. Paradis.

—World peace, said Mr. Chung.

—Make it something doable, said Mr. Paradis. You must be some kind of intellectual.

—Money, then.

—I can do that. I can get you money, but large amounts I'll have to steal.

—A raise?

—Three wishes and you want a raise? If it was me, I would go for good furniture, but a raise I can get you. You got a raise.

—A car.

—Buy it with the raise.

—There's nothing else.

—A new couch? A dining-room set? Something Moroccan?

—Whatever, said Mr. Chung.

And when he returned from work that night, his small apartment was lavishly decorated, filled with French furniture from the reign of one of the later Louis. There was scarcely room to maneuver. Mr. Paradis sat blinking on a red-velvet Louis XVI love seat.

—Did you steal this? Mr. Chung asked.

—No chance, said Mr. Paradis. And seeing how well set up you are, what do you need me for, eh?

—Yes, said Mr. Chung.

—Good furniture at a good price, said Mr. Paradis. That's what Heaven's about.

Mr. Paradis began to fade away, scratching himself here and there as he went. The sound of dry leaves remained even after he was gone, and the apartment smelled of wet earth, a smell that hung about for days, as there were no windows that could be opened.

Later that night, when Mr. Paradis had disappeared for good, Mr. Chung gathered the lace antimacassars that were draped on the furniture and threw them down the garbage chute. Then, two hours before dawn, when he was certain he would not be seen, he cleared out every piece of furniture Mr. Paradis had left behind and put them in front of the apartment building for the garbage collectors. From that moment he felt confident his life would continue in peace until his death. And it did.

3.

In 1987 Mr. André Bennett of 128 Gloucester invented, or rather discovered, a solution to world hunger. He bred a plant that passes through the body as food does, but that, when defecated, reverts to its original color, shape, and consistency and can thus be replanted and harvested time and again. This was, to the majority of Ottawans, an interesting but unpalatable discovery. Very few could see how, without expert promotion, one might convince the poor and starving to eat what they had just expelled.

The plant itself was much like a Canadian thistle, with smaller but more profuse spikes and a flower that was bright red against its lime-green stalk. It was lovely to behold, like something from a harsh world, but it had not been tested. It had never been given to human beings, though it had sustained a colony of rats for a year before Mr. Bennett made his discovery public.

As might be expected, Mr. Bennett's discovery attracted the attention of men of ambition throughout the city. And the first to promise him significant gain was Reed Marshall. Mr. Bennett surrendered his fate and the fate of his plant to Mr. Marshall forthwith.

Mr. Marshall had political ambitions, and his first act was to announce his candidacy for the office of mayor. His platform was "An end to hunger in the valley." With the help of his brother, Frederic, the owner of a local radio station, he quickly disseminated his ideas throughout the city. His first task was to end hunger in

Ottawa, and through a radio contest the seven poorest families in town were discovered and given the privilege of being the first to eat what was now called Bennett's Flower.

Food Day, as it was promoted, was a hot afternoon in July. A spruce rostrum was built in Minto Park, just wide enough to accommodate the ninety members of the city's seven poorest families. Mr. Marshall spoke to the small crowd that had gathered. He spoke into a microphone set before the rostrum. Several young boys pulled at the black electric wires that lay twisted on the pavement. At the end of his speech, he presented Mr. Bennett to the crowd, and Mr. Bennett pulled the long lime-green stalks from a plastic bag and handed them to the people on the rostrum. Thus, it was the Andrés, McKenzies, O'Briens, Lafleurs, Chaputs, Laflèches, and St. Pierres who discovered that the plant did not grow *after* it had been consumed and defecated but *while* it was being digested. The plants grew in their stomachs, up through their esophagi and out of their mouths. The plants also grew downward into their intestines and out of their anuses.

Besides causing extreme discomfort, the growth of Bennett's Flower was phenomenal. Every hour, the family members had to bite off the tops of the plants as they grew from their mouths and to cut off with pruning shears the growth from their nether extremities. This meant they could not sleep, and when they did, as the children did, their agony was redoubled. The spikes along the stalks were, of course, a continual discomfort.

There was nothing to be done for them.

It was certain proof of Mr. Marshall's talent as a politician, however, that, acting quickly, he turned the disaster and the suffering of the poor to his own advantage. He personally saw to it that Mr. Bennett was reprimanded for his shoddy scientific methods. But he also spearheaded a campaign to ensure that funds be put aside for Bennett to continue his research on the plants, with a view to the discovery of a herbicide that might assuage the agonies of the humans from whom Bennett's Flower continued to grow.

—This research, he said, will surely be of comfort to the poor.

And, it might have been, were it not that every member of the seven families died of starvation long before any balm was concocted. Still, it was ennobling to see the thin and naked poor, the Andrés, McKenzies, O'Briens, Lafleurs, Chaputs, Laflèches, and St. Pierres, snipping or trying to snip the plants from the mouths of their children, as they continued to do until their own last breaths.

4.

Nothing would give up life:
Even the dirt kept breathing a small breath.

—THEODORE ROETHKE

When the cemetery on Montreal Road was dug up to make more room for the dead, there was a general outcry. A committee was formed to ensure that the bones and relics of our ancestors were treated with respect. To their dismay, they discovered that the cemetery was infested by a breed of worm until then unknown. The worms were lily-white, not more than an inch long, and narrow as pins. At their extremities, the worms had minute, bright-red spots. And, when they were touched or exposed to the light, they emitted short, sharp cries. The grave diggers, or Thanatory Engineers as they preferred, could not dig up a spadeful of earth without exhuming thousands of them. They made the soil look like contaminated feces.

Shortly after they were discovered, the committee chairman, a distant relative of a distinguished corpse, Mr. Alan Thomas of 128 Wurtemberg, picked up one of the worms with his wife's tweezers and put it in a glass vial he had brought for the purpose. He took it home to study. He put the vial down on the low, glass-topped table in the family room, and it was there that his five-year-old son Edward discovered it. Edward opened the vial and swallowed the worm. Two weeks later, the boy began to speak with authority on aesthetic matters and to write poetry. He wrote beautiful poetry.

—It's like he swallowed Wallace Stevens, his father said.

—More like Eliot, scholars said, but not so neurotic.

—Still, an expert on child psychology remarked, there is no necessary connection between the worm and the poetry. The child was a prodigy with or without the Gravedigger's Worm.

To prove him wrong, Mr. Thomas swallowed one of the worms himself. With the same results: after two weeks, he began to write accomplished poetry.

—The father writes like Baudelaire, scholars said, but not so neurotic.

—Worms have nothing to do with it, a psychologist remarked. The father was obviously a poet before this business with the graveyard.

In any case, within months both the father and the son began to acquire renown for their work. (That is, they were published and sometimes admired, but they were generally treated with the contempt professionals reserve for those to whom things come too easily. And then, so few people cared for poetry, and even fewer could distinguish good verse from bad. They were called the Worms, père et fils.) These were their happy days. They lasted two full months. The Thomases wrote like demons.

Unfortunately, their bodies were hosts to the annelids. After three months they were infested. There were worms dangling and crying from their noses and ears and eyes and mouths. Whenever they moved, worms dropped from them. And, when the pain of being eaten alive became unbearable and they were confined to their beds, the worms infested their bedsheets. The noise the worms made was itself agonizing, like cries of schoolchildren heard from a distance.

After six months, they were both dead. Their corpses were white as marble, but their hands and feet were ash gray. The hair on their bodies was brittle as desiccated pine needles. The nails had fallen from their fingers and toes, and their skin was light as paper. When the pathologists cut into them, millions of worms, exposed to the light, began to cry out.

The bodies of the Thomases were taken out and burned.

The worms themselves also died out. They died when exhumed. And, when the reconstruction of the cemetery was completed they were annihilated, or seemed to be, and it was not possible to conduct any further experiments.

5.

On the 11th of January this year, all of the windows in the old fire hall on Sunnyside cracked. It was a cold and unusually dry night; so dry it was thought the dryness itself had cracked the windows. There were delicate threads of glass, some as long and thin as transparent hairs, scattered over the floor inside the hall. The shards were swept up with hard-bristle brooms, and a dance scheduled for the following night went on as planned.

Martine Beauchamp and her friends attended the dance together, six fourteen-year-old girls accompanied by Madame Florence Gru, Martine's grandmother. The heat inside the fire hall had been turned up to compensate for the cracked windows, so the air in the dance hall was as dry as straw in a drought. The girls took up positions against one of the walls. At the opposite end of the room, the young men stood together.

An older man, perhaps twenty years old, with light-blue eyes and extremely white skin, asked Martine to dance. He asked politely, and Martine's grandmother gave her permission.

—Mais oui, said Madame Gru. On voit qu'il est cultivé.

And the two of them danced all night, finding that they had much to talk about.

The man's only indiscretion came when they were about to part for the evening. He put two of his fingers into Martine's mouth and pressed on her tongue. But Madame Gru was willing to believe that this had been accidental, or else a new custom with the well-bred. (Martine was even more surprised than her grandmother, but not unpleasantly. His fingers had been dry as paper, and her tongue had stuck to them lightly.)

The following week there was another dance at the fire hall. Martine and her friends went eagerly, dragging Madame Gru with them. And this night was identical to the first. When Mr. Highsmith put up his two fingers to touch her, Martine smiled and opened her mouth slightly. He said good night after they had danced and laughed for hours.

It was on the way home from the dance, as she and her friends talked of everything but Mr. Highsmith, about whom she was too excited to speak, that Martine realized she had forgotten her gloves. The girls and Madame Gru had already reached the bank of the river.

The river was not completely frozen. Near its center a smooth black strand of water flowed in the ice and snow. The moon was white in the cloudless sky, and it was as she looked down at her hands that Martine saw that she had forgotten her gloves. Asking her friends to take her grandmother home, she walked back to the fire hall alone.

As she neared the building, Martine saw Mr. Highsmith leave. He walked away from her, toward Bank Street, and at the corner he turned toward the canal. Martine followed him, anxious to say good night again, but instead of walking along Echo Drive, Mr. Highsmith cut across the snow-covered driveway and walked to the back of the monastery.

Behind the monastery was a large, stone replica of a church, the size of a small cottage. It had been built to keep the bodies of priests who died. Their remains lay on a bier for two days before burial so that the confreres of the dead could pay their final respects. Mr. Highsmith entered the building directly, and by the time Martine looked in at the window to see what he was doing, Mr. Highsmith had already stripped Father Alfred Bertrand's corpse of its shroud and he had begun to eat the priest's body.

Martine put her hand to the window to support herself, and when she did, the window creaked dryly and ice fell around her. Mr. Highsmith looked up, but by then she was already running. The snow on the monastery ground seemed deeper and colder and almost impassable.

In the days that followed, Martine avoided company. She told no one what she had seen. To her mother and her grandmother she seemed to be pining for her young man. They encouraged her to go out, and when, a month later, there was a community dance at the fire hall, they insisted she attend.

—Vas y, ma chère, said her mother, smiling, et sans chaperon.

—Oui, said Madame Gru, ce monsieur Highsmith est la politesse même.

Her friends teased her and tried to encourage her, but she hid in their midst until they came to the hall.

Mr. Highsmith approached her immediately, and he was so friendly, Martine believed he had not seen her or heard her at the monastery. As they walked to the dance floor, he took her missing gloves from his suit pocket.

—You must have forgotten these, he said.

—Yes, thank you, Martine answered.

—The last time we saw each other was some time ago, said Mr. Highsmith.

—Yes, said Martine.

—You followed me to the chapel.

—No.

—What was I doing there?

—I don't know.

Mr. Highsmith put up his two fingers and forced them into her mouth.

—Very well, he said. When you return home tonight you will find your grandmother dead.

And then they danced. Mr. Highsmith held her so close she could not move, and to the people around them they seemed happy. At the end of the night, when she returned home, Martine found her grandmother dead.

In Martine's bedroom there is a window that looks out on a garden, and beyond the garden, there is a curtain of pine trees. As she looked out the window several weeks later, when her grandmother had been buried for some time, she saw Mr. Highsmith come through the trees. He called out to her.

—How's your memory, my dear? Did you see me in the chapel that night?

—No, Martine answered.

—Did you see what I was doing?

—No.

—Tut tut, he said. Your mother is dead before sunrise.

She moved away from the window, and she began to cry, but in the morning her mother was dead.

Some time after her mother's death, Mr. Highsmith knocked at her front door. Martine, alone, opened the door to him, and before she could close it, he put a foot on the threshold.

—And how is your mother? he said, smiling. I was wondering, my little bitch, did you see me in the chapel that night?

—No.

—Did you see what I was doing?

—No.

—Well, said Mr. Highsmith, time is finite. If you do

not tell someone, anyone, what it was you saw that night, you will die within a week. But whoever you tell will die.

And he disappeared. And from that moment, Martine began to die slowly, feeling the life pulled out of her as if it were a strand of hair pulled through her fingers. She did not know what to do, but when the pain of dying overcame her, she threw open her bedroom window and shouted out what it was she had seen. She told everything to the garden.

That's how I heard the story.

A curse on anyone who reads this.

· III ·

André

The Third Terrace

La main est l'un des animaux de l'homme . . .

—Francis Ponge

1.

I was born in Ottawa, in 1957. My family was middle-class. My parents had raised themselves from the gutter and hoped to get even farther from it through their children. To that end, I was given a good education. After high school I went to the University of Ottawa, where I studied literature, for a term, and then art history.

As far as I can recall, I was unexceptional in every way. I was plump and socially graceless. My mind had only two speeds: Dead Slow and Stop. (I did have beautiful hands, but I wasn't especially proud of them. Most of the time, I wore loose-fitting gloves.)

When I graduated I discovered I was ill equipped for the world. Being able to tell Bosch from Brueghel doesn't open many doors, and I wasn't always able to do even that much. So, with the grudging support of my parents, I decided to become an artist. I would learn to paint.

I had only one influence: Piero della Francesca. It was Piero this and Piero that. I lived, ate, and shat Renaissance perspective. (Not that I ever mastered it. Most of my canvases ended up black from the false lines I drew on them, but I persevered.)

After a year of devotion to painting, I had become somewhat more adept, but I was out of step with the Art of my time. I did exhibit two of my "blackened" della Francescas in a school gymnasium, and for a second there I was almost popular. An art critic called me a "bleak ironist," and that gave my reputation a little fillip. The *Ottawa Citizen* doesn't carry much weight, though, and in the end, my father bought both of my paintings after haggling about the price.

Indigent, unwilling to return home, I put painting aside two years after I'd taken it up. And so it was that, at twenty-five, I went to work at the Café Wim.

It was there that I met Mr. Kingsley.

It was a Saturday in June of 1982 and I wasn't wearing gloves. Mr. Kingsley sat by the bow window and ate his cheese on rusk. We spoke briefly about the weather, the stink of the canal, and the state of the federation: the usual thing between diner and waiter. When he got up to leave, however, he casually mentioned that he found my hands attractive. He asked if I had ever thought of working in film.

Now, as he had mentioned my hands, I knew what kind of "film" he had in mind. I had been to Hull, and I had seen a few erotic movies. (I'd even enjoyed them, without taking them too seriously.) Still, I said yes, and he put his business card faceup on the table between us:

Mr. Charles Kingsley
White Films Production Co.
58 Denison Avenue,
Toronto, Ontario

—If you can get the money together, he said, come see me in Toronto.

I don't remember what impressed me most about Mr. Kingsley. His courtesy? His business card? His natty blue suit? It was all very appealing. I remember thinking that, with a few dollars in my pocket, I'd be able to afford the things I needed for my Art: paint and canvas, brushes and turpentine.

—Does it pay well? I asked.

—Of course, he said.

And that was it. I would make a few erotic films and then retire to my true calling: Art, Piero, and the Renaissance.

I hadn't managed to save a lot of money, but I had enough for a round-trip ticket to Toronto. Moreover, I was so confident of success I left my job at Wim's, packed my belongings in a suitcase, put my paintings in storage, and lit out for the city. There was even music in my head as I rode the bus: "East St. Louis Toodleoo."

. . .

I arrived in Toronto on a Friday afternoon and went directly to the offices of White Films. I asked for Mr. Kingsley, but Mr. Kingsley was not in. Instead, I was taken to Mr. Bultmann, ushered into his office, suitcase and all.

—Just put your hands up on the desk, will you? he said.

When I did, his face turned beet red, and he began to perspire.

—I think you'll be wonderful, he said.

He looked away, pushed the papers on his desk aside, and took a Kleenex from a brightly colored box.

—We've got a little something planned for this evening. Can you start this evening?

—Of course.

—Good. Have you got a place to stay? I mean, until then . . . Are you set up?

—I just got in. I guess I could walk around until six . . .

—Don't have to walk around at all, he said. Stay here. Just throw your suitcase in the corner and relax.

He wasn't an intimidating man. Short, bespectacled, and clothed in polyester is what he was. An arc of neatly trimmed red hair framed the liver spots on his pate, and he rubbed the top of his ear with the Kleenex.

—I think I'll walk around, I said.

It was my first experience of Toronto, and I couldn't help thinking of it in terms of fabric. The clouds were flocculent, the leaves linen, and the streets seemed to unfurl.

At six o'clock I returned to Mr. Bultmann's office. Mr. Bultmann was there to meet me. With him was Thomas Merton (better known as Dick Clump), the director of what was to be my first loop.

—You feeling okay? Mr. Bultmann asked. You don't want to rest up a little? Wash your hands? It could help put you in the mood. You got to watch the psychology thing . . . in my experience . . .

Mr. Merton silently appraised my claws.

—Course, we don't shoot here, Mr. Bultmann continued. Here's strictly business. You're going to King Street. That's where the action is . . . You know, I really envy the young . . . I'd have the stuff if I was younger, don't you think?

He pushed his hands from their burrows. They were wrinkled, spotted, and covered in moles. Mr. Merton looked away and coughed.

The loop was a thing called *The Master's Larder*. It lasted twenty minutes. I was costumed in black plague–era robes. The only part of my body clearly visible were my hands.

I played a manservant who, when the lord and lady of the manor have gone, picks the lock of the kitchen larder. Inside, there are jars of tangerine honey and piles of bone-white, brushed-cotton tablecloths. For twenty minutes I dipped my hands in honey and pulled the cloths from their hardwood shelves and then folded them again, meticulously.

Because this was the first time I had done anything so explicit for the camera, there were only two others present: the cameraman and the director. Mr. Merton gave me careful instructions as we filmed:

—Put your fingers in that top fold. That's it . . . let them linger. Now, pull them out, slowly. That's it. Slower . . . crumple it a little. A little more. Crumple it. Now hold it in your knuckles. Pull it through. Slowly . . . slowly . . .

And that's how I made my first erotic film.

All of this must seem incredible to those of you who don't know the industry. It was certainly incredible to me. I was being paid to reveal my hands and fingers, as well as something I had no idea I possessed: my "erotic nature."

Now, where had this "nature" come from? Where had it been hidden? How had strangers like Kingsley, Bultmann, and Merton detected it so easily? It took me a full year to discover the reality of its existence, and the discovery itself was something of an accident:

I was filming my first feature, *Sheets in Aqaba*. The story was minimal, as they usually are. In this one, Lawrence of Arabia, played by Mark Lombardo, has various erotic adventures in the Middle East. I played Berty, Lawrence's close friend. During the first half hour I am captured by angry Arabs, beaten, and left for dead in the desert. There, I am rescued by Fatima, a wife of the sultan. She smuggles me into the sultan's harem, wraps me in red robes, and nurses me back to health. Our first sex scene has us shyly choosing the bolt of cloth that will be used for my disguise. Our hands linger in the folds of yellow silk, and then I am rescued by Lawrence.

As I said, I was not yet aware of my "nature." I was professional. My hands and fingers belonged to other people: the producer, the director, whomever. But, during this scene with Fatima and Lawrence, I began to feel a strange excitement. There was something about Mark Lombardo's fingers. They were graceful, thin, and pale, but one of the joints of his left index finger had been broken, and this finger curved slightly to one side no matter how he held it. For the first time, I was captivated by the beauty of an actor's hands.

At that moment I understood what these films were all about. I saw what it was Kingsley had seen in me, and I knew why I had come to Toronto: I had been guided from below.

Naturally, I began to struggle against myself. After *Aqaba* I spent all my money on rolls of canvas, pots of gesso, and tube after tube of Winsor Newtons. I began to paint again, passionately, though instead of returning to della Francesca, I immersed myself in neo-Expressionism. (Now, it was Mimmo Paladino I imitated, and the portraits I did were so thick the paint fell off in clumps as it dried.) I did everything I could to serve my "higher calling," as if that might protect me from the intrusion of my sexual nature.

Then, while filming *Three Sheets to the Wind*, I had my first orgasm on-screen.

I'm not sure what happened. *Three Sheets* was no different from any of the other films I'd done. It was set on a pirate ship, the *Blue Flame*, and I played an Englishman captured by buccaneers.

The pirates confine me and the two women who are my daughters to a dreary cabin below deck. In the cabin there is a hard, unmattressed bed, a wobbly wooden table, and, on a wall, a tattered map of the seas. My daughters help me undress to my nightshirt. Then I help them undress down to their shifts and stays. Finally, I cover them with a damp, moth-eaten blanket.

The women in this scene, Molly Brand and Irene Buttress, had exquisite hands. Molly's fingers were short and thick, with long nails that she kept carefully trimmed and red as poppies. The lines on her palms were deep and rust brown. Irene's hands were delicate, almost tiny. Her palms were white, smooth as a porcelain bowl. Together, the women unbuttoned my vest, slipping the pearl circles carefully through the woven eyes.

The sound of their hands in the fabric, the light of the candles on the table, the smell of wool: it was all too much for me. I shivered like a Mexican hairless, and then I came.

I understand how sordid this must sound, but it has happened to everyone at some time. The cameras were stopped. The actors waited as I cleaned myself. The director said:

—Take it from the unbuttoning.

And we went on as though nothing had happened.

Something *had* happened.

After that, I could not stop thinking of fingers and fabric. I was fascinated by them. In the morning, before work, I would stare at my palms and fingers. I imagined myself in minor accidents in which my fingers were crushed beneath the wheels of a car or a shopping cart. I saw my fingers penetrating tight places: a closed flower; a moist underarm; a hole in dry, white plaster; a brass socket.

Then, about a month after *Three Sheets to the Wind*, I began to have sex with the prostitutes on Church. It was with them that I first experienced the joy of linseed and cotton, burlap and Vaseline.

My first encounter with a prostitute was so squalid, it's a wonder I ever went back. It was night and I was walking along Church near Carleton. It was raining hard, but as I passed the CBC a young man, his body almost completely hidden in white silk, asked me if I was lonely. I said I was a little lonely and he pushed one of his hands out from the silk sleeves. It was his left hand, and he was missing two fingers. One, the index, was cut off at the first joint. The other, the ring, was a lovely stump, cut off just above the knuckle. They were both old injuries. Flesh had grown over the bone. I was captivated. I asked how much. Fifty dollars for silk, one hundred dollars for cotton in linseed, and two hundred dollars for oiled burlap. Then, having settled on burlap, we hailed a cab and went to what looked like a flop-house, on Dundas. It turned out to be a "hotel." I paid the clerk twenty-five dollars for the room.

The room itself was small and windowless. A tiny bathroom, little more than a sink beneath a mirror, was off to one side. A narrow door in one of the walls hid a small closet in which there were heaps of fabric and tubs of liquid. I stood in the center of the room as he pulled out a bolt of dry burlap that smelled of peat. So far, so good.

The problem was he was businesslike. Everything went by quickly. After I paid him, he allowed me only a brief look at his hands. (His "good" hand was unexceptional.) He rubbed them over his robe as though he were cold, turning them this way and that perfunctorily. Then he unbuckled my pants and yanked them down. I had to take down my own underwear. It was like a visit to the doctor's. He picked up the burlap, gave it to me, took a tub of axle grease from the closet, and set it down between us. He said:

—Go ahead.

But I was so unimpressed I was barely erect. It was only as he rubbed the grease into the burlap that I became excited. There he was, in white silk, his fingers blackened in axle grease, playing in the folds of burlap. And, when I put my own hands into the tub of cool grease, nature took its course. I mean: I came.

It was this encounter that began my obsession with injuries, with the kind of deformities that weren't shown on film. From that night on I sought out damaged goods.

There were all sorts of injuries, of course. Some of my lovers had lost fingers in accidents. Others born with their defects. (One in particular was magnificent: she had only two fingers on her right hand. Her hand was only half its normal length, and the fingers seemed to sprout from the middle of her palm. Together, we rubbed linseed oil on a velvet dress; the most exquisite sex I've ever had.) Still others had damaged their hands with heavy weights or blunt instruments. There was something about the hopelessly unique that excited me, and after a while nothing else would do.

I gradually lost interest in the people around me and in the films I was making. In the evening I would walk along Church or Jarvis appraising the outstretched hands, the minor injuries, admiring the way the prostitutes held themselves: bent forward in their robes, their hands level with my waist.

It was six months after all this that I had the first of my two accidents:

I was on Church Street. It was midwinter and dark, and the prostitutes were gorgeous, beneath the streetlights, in their colored robes.

A woman in a bright-yellow caftan, her face veiled, put out her right hand.

—Company? she said.

Her hand was beautiful. It was almost precisely maimed. Of her fingers there remained only stubs, pinched at the tips as though they had been cut with secateurs. Her thumb was undamaged, but it twitched like a frog's leg in electric current. I couldn't tell what kind of accident she'd had.

—Sure, I said.

We took a taxi along Dundas, past the hotels in Chinatown, past the places I was used to, but I didn't notice how far afield we'd gone. I was entranced. Her caftan was yellow as a sunflower and soft. Her hands smelled of vanilla. When we got out of the cab, I had no idea where we were, though the neighborhood was no seedier than I expected.

We went into a narrow, grimy building. At the front desk was a young man who was bald, save for a circular patch of hair that drooped from the side of his head.

—Twenty for the room, he said.

He barely looked up from the small television on the counter. When he had my money he said:

—Sixteen.

We went up the stairs, the woman and I. Bedsheets hung from the banister like laundry. The stairwell walls were splotched and stained, and lime green where the paint had fallen off.

Number 16 was large, square, and white. A window, draped with lace curtains, was on one wall. There was no bathroom. A narrow bed stood in the center of the room, as though we were going to reproduce. I didn't notice the closet until a little later.

The woman pulled a tub of Vaseline and a large piece of burlap out from under the bed. The burlap had been used. It was gummy, black, and sucked as she unfolded it. It was so exciting watching her peel the cloth open, I pulled down my pants and underwear myself.

And then, as though the wind had taken it, the closet door banged against the wall. Someone said:

—Hello, sailor.

And the woman got up to wipe her hands on my coat.

—Pull up your pants, she said.

There were now two men in the room with us. One of them held a lead pipe by two fingers, as though it were a rat's tail. I was terrified, and it was like every other time I've been terrified: my head began to hum and all the colors in the room grew unbearably bright.

I reached down to pull up my pants. The man nearest me kicked my ribs. I fell over.

—That's the position, he said.

The other one sat on my arm.

—What's he worth? he said.

I said:

—Please, take whatever you want.

The woman had gone through my pockets and taken the money from my wallet, but she wasn't happy. She stepped on my hand. I cried out, and almost immediately the man with the lead pipe struck the side of my head.

From there I don't remember much. I stopped moving and fled to the places inside: my mother's voice calling me home, someone whispering, the sound of bedsheets as I slid out of them, my hands on a kitten's belly, stones in summer, the river at night . . .

When I woke, the hotel clerk was above me, gently slapping the side of my face.

—Some party, he said.

I was where they'd left me, my pants around

my ankles, the blood on the side of my face like a second skin.

—It's time to go, said the clerk.

He helped me to my feet, but I could neither dress myself nor move my arms.

—You need help? You want a taxi?

I wanted a taxi, among other things, but there was no money, so I went down the stairs with my coat on my head, my pants held up by my arms.

2.

Carpals, metacarpals, phalanges: so many bones to break. My elbow had only been knocked out of joint, but my left hand was truly mangled.

During the months it took me to recover the use of my limb, I reflected on what had happened to me. What I couldn't understand was *why* it had happened. Had I sinned? Had I earned the woman's enmity? Was it destiny?

I had been a young man with beautiful hands. I might have modeled. I might have found work in legitimate films. I might even have painted, but would any of these other lives have changed my fate? It was possible, wasn't it, that every direction held the germ of my downfall? Perhaps the woman and her accomplices had been born with my image as part of their collective memory. They had been God driven, conscious only of His will, a three-person vengeance . . .

That's the kind of thing I thought about, for months. In fact, I did way too much thinking. At first I blamed myself for what had happened, and then society, and then myself, and then my assailants, and then myself, and then God (in whom I did not quite believe). I was bitter that my looks had been spoiled, and then grateful, bitter, grateful, bitter, bitter, bitter. It took me six months to dredge up thousands of small questions, and then a few more to realize I couldn't answer them alone.

So, my recuperation was frustrating, dull, and exhilarating. I mean, my life was reduced to basics. I did little. I could barely cook for myself. I couldn't dress properly. I stayed in bed. That was the dull part. The exhilaration came from anger. While my mind was at work on the metaphysical questions, my imagination spewed out pictures of violence. I saw myself assaulting my attackers with a wide variety of implements: a pool cue, a gun, a bread knife, an automobile, garden shears. Wherever I was, whatever I was thinking, visions of carnage would overtake me and my heart would race. After months of that, I was fairly excited by the idea of vengeance.

Not that I was vengeance driven. It wasn't so simple. I also wanted to speak to the woman and her accomplices, to make them understand. I mean, I was civilized. I wanted dialogue. Still, I bought a gun and a permit and I went back to Church and Carleton.

Six months had passed since my accident. I was now wiry and cheddar-faced. I kept my arm close to my body, tucked in. On the street I tried to walk in a consistently different manner, limping at every step, throwing my right leg out in front of me. It was unlikely anyone would recognize me, but I wanted to be sure.

My recuperation had been dull, but the next few weeks were excruciating. Time stopped. I spent hours on Church and on Jarvis.

I wasn't looking for a woman in a yellow caftan. That would have been risky, there were so many yellow caftans about that year. Instead, I was looking for her hands. I inspected each and every hand presented to me. Here, the fingers were similar, but the thumb didn't shake. There, the thumb shook, but there were too many fingers. Night after night it was the same thing: limping patience. And then a woman's voice asked:

—Company?

With just the right inflection. And put out a hand with the right number of stubs, pinched at the tips, with a thumb that quivered in a peculiar way.

All that I had been through, all of my emotions, flooded my imagination, and for a second there I was utterly confused.

She was wearing a hooded white robe over her winter clothes. She didn't even bother to look up at me. She bent forward, with some difficulty, and proffered her gorgeous hand. You could see she hadn't lost any sleep over my misfortune, and I felt a sort of pity, as though what I was about to do were more cruel than what had been done to me.

I leaned forward to look at her face. She bent down further to avoid me. She held her hand up and went down as far as she could without falling. So it was that, with my head almost touching the pavement, I first saw her face.

It wasn't the most propitious angle. The shadows were a bit distracting and the blood had rushed to her face, but there was something, something in her long, brown hair, black eyebrows, thin nose, and flared nostrils, her high cheekbones.

—Want company or what?

—No, thank you, I said.

And straightened up slowly and limped off, making sure to casually inspect the hands of the other prostitutes along the way.

At the first corner, I turned west, then north on Yonge, east on Carleton, and south on Church so that I was on my way back to her.

It wasn't as though I had a plan. I mean, I wanted to kill her, but there were details to consider. I could:

1. Shoot her on the spot, without giving her a dressing-down.

   That was unacceptable.

2. Give her a dressing-down, and then shoot her.

   That was awkward.

3. Accompany her to a hotel, dress her down, then shoot her.

   The best option, though she might recognize me en route and jump from the car.

4. Dress her down, accompany her to the hotel, and shoot her.

Which would call for the kind of brutal persuasion I wasn't sure I possessed.

5. Shoot her nonfatally, accompany her to the hotel, and dress her down. Which introduced the novel idea of a nonfatal shooting and all the mechanical precision that implied.

6. Dress her down, shoot her, and then take her to the hotel.
Out of the question, for technical reasons.

7. Shoot her, dress her down, and then take her to the hotel.
Out of the question, and for similar reasons . . .

Aside from all that, there were her accomplices to consider. Where were they? (I kept the gun in my right coat pocket. The bullets I kept in my left, for fear I might shoot myself. Would I have time to clean the lint from the bullets, put them in the chamber, and then squeeze off three precise shots? I didn't think so.) And there was her face. It had been a mistake to look so closely.

So, I returned to her without any real plan of action. This time, however, I crossed to the opposite side of the street as soon as I had her in view. I was about a block away, by a maple tree, when I stopped to watch her.

As far as I could tell, she did nothing out of the ordinary. She stood patiently, talking to no one. Then, when a certain type of pedestrian approached, she would bend forward, present her hand, and, if there were no interest, return to her place on the pavement.

Once or twice she looked up and her face was bathed in streetlight. Once, she looked in my direction but without purpose, without interest. It was not one of her successful nights.

We had spoken to each other around midnight. At four in the morning, she took off her robe, put on gloves, and walked away. I myself was exhausted, having been approached by countless men and women looking for a good time, so I was happy to follow her.

She turned east on Queen, south on Ontario, east again, south again, then entered an apartment building just shy of Parliament. Not once had she bothered to turn around. She hadn't the slightest idea she was being followed, no idea that she might be followed. It was proof that she'd been sleeping the sleep of the Just. Had my bruised and broken body left the least impression on her soul? Was there a groat's worth of regret to be had from her? Did she have an inkling, even in her most private moments, that I might deserve vengeance? No, not at all, not a bit.

It was one of those winter nights when it makes no sense to be outdoors. There was an inch of wet snow on the ground. The moon was a platinum smudge, let's say, and the street was full of that peculiar light that makes everything appear vivid and two-dimensional. If I had been thinking straight, I would have gone home. Instead, I found an alley between two houses facing her apartment building. I walked up and down quietly, or sat on an empty garbage can from which I'd cleaned the snow.

This night, I was to have my most thrilling philosophical moment. Perhaps it was the cold. In any case, ass in a can, I seemed to glimpse a purpose to the universe: everything is pushed from behind or held in place. The stars couldn't move. The sun was held fast; the earth was constrained. All we could do, any of us, was spin. All that we want, and all we pursue, gives the illusion of movement, of liberty. There is no movement, no liberty, only local phenomena of such paltry significance it's a wonder we get out of bed for them.

It was quite a touching moment. I felt briefly at one with the stars. I might even have discovered deeper meaning to life, but it was cold. I jumped up and returned to thoughts of the woman and her accomplices, loading and unloading my gun in the dark.

At one o'clock the following afternoon, she stumbled out of the building. By that time, I was cold, wet, and on the verge of hallucination. She was in a navy-blue coat, a Peruvian tuque, and white gloves, but I recognized her. I took up the chase.

And this was the longest, most confusing day of my life. I followed her in and out of fabric stores. She lingered in pharmacies. She sat for hours in a coffee shop, for minutes in a restaurant. Someone called her Maureen. She drank coffee. She ate fried eggs, boiled potatoes, dill pickles, and toast. I couldn't have predicted her activity if my life depended on it. (Of course, I'm not sure how much of my confusion was self-inflicted. My poor, frazzled brain saw only chaos. I can't tell if there was more to see.) The only thing I knew for certain was that she had no idea I was with her. I could have shot her anytime.

That night, I was with Dante on the third terrace of purgatory, my thoughts at one with the course of the stars. I was clear as to the fate of several souls: mine, "Maureen's," those of her accomplices.

—Company? she asked as I approached.

—Sure, I said.

And felt almost holy as we stepped into a taxi and drove along Dundas, away from the safer places.

The "hotel" was the same. There was an older, gray-haired man at the front desk. He put out his hand, without looking up from the television on the counter. I paid him.

—Sixteen, he said.

It seemed to me the same sheets hung over the banister, and the walls were just as dirty. It was all very interesting. I was myself, but I was also an angel of death. "Maureen" was doomed.

We went calmly into number 16. She approached the bed, bent down to pull out the grease and burlap I'd asked for, and it was then that I took the gun from my pocket, faced the closet, and fired four shots into it. (It wasn't easy, you know. I wasn't prepared for the recoil. Those four shots took a good fifteen seconds, but I managed to hit the closet where I wanted.)

There was a *clump*, like a body falling to the floor, but it didn't sound as if it came from the closet, not really. It sounded distant. "Maureen" cried out in surprise, stood up, and moved away from me. I said:

—Don't move.

But she kept moving toward the window. I fired at her feet, to get her attention. Then, I took four lint-covered bullets from my coat pocket. One of them fell to the floor, but I managed to put the others in their chambers. That fallen bullet was a giveaway: you could see I was upset.

Outside, there was a great deal of confusion: heavy footsteps and rushing about. It reminded me of a time when I had broken an expensive vase and my parents had come running.

—You remember me? I asked.

—No, "Maureen" answered.

This wasn't at all what I'd expected. It was too diffuse. I was upset, but I wasn't really angry anymore, not at "Maureen." It seemed to me as though God Himself didn't care if she or her partners lived or died.

—Take off your clothes, I said.

—You're not going to fuck me, are you? she asked.

I looked into her eyes and saw nothing of interest. She wasn't even there.

—Shut up and keep them on, then, I said.

But she went on undressing, prepared for the worst, though the thought of reproductive contact hadn't crossed my mind. I'd merely wanted to keep her busy while I dressed her down.

She stood naked before me, her left arm up, to cover her small breasts, her right hand over her pubis, her thin body bent forward, her face looking up at mine. It was repulsive. If she'd said anything, anything at all, I'm sure I'd have shot her, just to get it over with.

The problem was I couldn't decide what to do. I didn't know *how* to dress her down. I had too many things to say, but my mind was stuck on "Do something. Do something." So, when I shot her in the leg it really was an accident, my second accident, or something very like it. The gun went off. "Maureen" cried out in misery and fell to the floor.

I won't pretend that any of this made sense to me, that I felt relief, that all the tessera of my life suddenly formed a precise image. That didn't happen. I was as confused then as I am now. It occurred to me that "Maureen" would get splinters if she lay on the floor too long, then I walked out.

I left the hotel undisturbed, a police car passing by me as I hailed a cab. I don't remember what I was thinking, but it can't have been much.

3.

The moment I fired into the closet, all of Nature turned away from me. The spirit went out of the things around me. (I can't describe it any other way: the spirit of things receded, like the tide going out.) I was like a stranger to the world: the floor would take my steps, but no more; the walls supported my weight, but unwillingly; lights would illuminate and hinges turn, but despite me, not for me. I could have put my hand in flame without having it burn, or breathed underwater without drowning. The rules no longer applied to me, though instead of feeling liberated I longed for the old order. I wanted to drown.

To put it plainly: my soul no longer recognized its home. For two years, it has followed one path, while my body has followed another.

I wish I had the words to explain what I've been through, but there's so much I don't understand and still more I don't want to face. I could explain it all as Fate, I suppose, but that's not right. I could speak of accidents, but that's not it either. What I need is a common language for body and soul, a language to articulate these lost years. I don't hold out much hope for it.

Still, all of this has been sinking back into the mire for some time now. I think of "Maureen" much less often. I have my nightmares of her face no more than once a month. Gradually, the world is coming back to me. (This morning, for instance, I burned my toast and the smell almost brought me to life.) I've been building a bridge between now and then, without knowing.

I first became aware of this bridge while filming *Broken Knuckles*. I was rehearsing a scene with Irene Buttress. Our fingers looked beautiful as we rubbed freshly tanned leather. The little finger of her right hand was bent to a forty-five-degree angle, and I suddenly remembered how much pleasure her hands had given me, how pure it was to be in contact with rough fabric.

That was a few months ago.

These days, I try to keep my right hand before the camera. (My left does have a certain je ne sais quoi, but I can't stand to have it filmed.) I earn a living, but I'll never go back to Church Street to admire the fingers.

It's the price I pay.

Horse

1. MY MOTHER DIES

In 1987 I had two recurring dreams. I was not living in my mother's house on Riverside, and I was at peace with myself (I think), and I must have been perplexed by these nightmares. In the first:

I am walking along Bank Street. It is winter, and the snow is deep. I understand I am near Fifth Avenue because I recognize the ambience, though I can't identify the buildings around me. The snow falls and sticks to my eyelashes. My shoes squeak and crunch on the ground. I hear a church bell ringing, not like the carillons in the vicinity, but loud and clear, as though someone were striking a large bell directly behind me. I stop to count the toll, but I get no farther than 10 before I lose track. This I do several times before giving up and thinking: There's something wrong with the bell. Once I stop counting, I recognize the bar across the street. It is a bar I rarely frequent, but I am cold so I cross the street to reach it. From outside, I hear the sound of people enjoying themselves. I am relieved at the prospect of company, but on entering I find the room almost deserted. Behind the bar, a tall man with blue eyes stands waiting. We exchange rather formal pleasantries before he asks me what I want. His face is moonish and his flesh is white as dough. I think to myself: The light is bad. I take whiskey and sit at the bay window that once looked out onto Bank but that now faces another street, and I realize the bar has moved. My table is covered in dust through which ticks have burrowed trails that, seen from above, resemble a written word. After a time, during which I can still hear the sound of people laughing, I get up and go to the bathroom. The bartender watches in disgust as I approach. When I ask him for directions, he holds his nose and points to a stairwell to the basement. Beside the stairwell, at a table for two, sits a man I had not noticed. For some reason, it doesn't strike me as odd that his head is not on his shoulders but on the table in front of him. The head, which he steadies with one hand, looks up at me as I pass and smiles politely. On his tabletop the ticks have carved:

At the bottom of the stairs I see that the hallway goes off in two directions. "Straight ahead," the bartender shouts, and I am led by voices that I assume come from the men's washroom. Inside the washroom are half a dozen men. They are sitting on chairs in a semicircle, and like the man upstairs, they are headless. Their heads are on their laps. They stare at me as I enter.

—What does he want? someone asks.

—Grâce, vous vous méprenez! says someone else.

And the heads on their laps begin to laugh and chatter.

—Assassin, I say, va perpétrer ailleurs des crimes que tu crois impardonnables.

Which causes them to choke with laughter. I don't understand what's funny, and my lack of understanding annoys them. They begin to grimace and threaten. A hand holding a man's head by the hair comes over my shoulder. The nose touches mine. The head makes threatening faces and tells me to get out. Instead of backing out, I bite the nose and sink my teeth into its cartilage. The hand holding the head releases it. The head begins to plead beneath me.

—Let me go. You're hurting me. Please . . .

And it is at this moment, feeling my neck bend with the weight, that I wake.

Naturally, I have no idea what these things mean, if they mean anything at all. I found this dream sinister and frightening, but as nothing untoward happens to me, I no longer know why.

As I said, I think I was at peace with myself. My mother's illness, which was terminal, had been a fact of life for so long it had ceased to be a source of distress. When she died that winter, I was even, perhaps a little, relieved she had been freed from her misery, or so I presume. (I presume about my state of mind, of course. My mother was certainly dead. She did not complain about the shroud, the casket, or the black roses at her funeral. Alive, she would have had legitimate grounds for complaint, and it was not like her to pass up a chance to berate me.)

After my mother's death, I stopped dreaming altogether, or stopped remembering my dreams. I had to take care of the million little details attendant on the ordering of an estate. I tagged all of the items in the house. Each tag had a number, and each number was noted on a page beside the item to which it corresponded. The floor lamp in the basement was number 1. A pair of socks found at the bottom of a trunk in the attic was number 5,000 and something. (Going through her property, I discovered the extent of my mother's confusion in the days before cancer put an end to her mobility: in almost all of the chests and drawers I discovered the dried lozenges of feces she had meant to hide from view.) Once this list was dressed, I called in the appraisers. I was dismayed to find that much of her property was of little value. The house itself, because it was on Riverside, near Pill Hill, was worth quite a bit, but I wanted to keep it. And when all that could be sold had been, I found myself in an unfurnished three-story house, parts of which I would have to rent out to support myself.

The part of the house in which I chose to live, the basement, was spacious. The floors were carpeted; the walls were white. There were several rooms, a bathroom, an L-shaped bedroom. I kept a single piece of furniture for myself: a narrow, iron-framed, rusty bed for which, being a link to my childhood, I still had affection. I also kept those photographs I could not sell and half a dozen letters my mother had written but neglected to mail.

The rest of the house—the rooms, their closets and corners, ceilings and floors—I came to know gradually. As with any place that has been inhabited, each room was unique. My mother's room, for instance, was "warm." Its walls were still spotted where her fingers had touched. I had given all of the rooms a thorough cleaning, but I had been, perhaps unconsciously (?), less assiduous in my mother's bedroom. Consequently, it smelled only faintly of Lysol and might have been called disheveled by a more conscientious char. The other rooms on the upper floors were less appealing, but I visited them as well, regularly. In all, there were:

> my mother's room (a)
> > (b) my sister's room
> the guest room (c)
> > (d) the living room
> the family room (e)
> > (f) the dining room

the spare bedroom (g)

(h) my mother's bathroom

the large bathroom (i)

(j) the entertainment room

the workroom (k)

(l) the boiler room

the basement bathroom (m)

(n) my bedroom

my father's office (o)

(p) the dance room

the kitchen (q)

(r) the bar

the foyer (s)

(t) the walk-in closet

mother's closet (u)

(v) the garage

the attic (w)

(x) the wine cellar

my younger sister's bedroom (y)

(z) the storage room

And one of my typical trajectories through the house might be called:

wmnovlzkjrioyqspdgxahtbeuc

And I would execute this trajectory, or some variant on it, four or five times a night, as a break from whatever I might be doing at the time.

2. LANARK

The second dream recurred as frequently as the first. Sometimes it preceded the first, and sometimes it followed it without my ever being able to understand the connection between them:

I am in my mother's house. I live there now. She has died and I am alone. I have been there for some time, and weeks pass. The weeks are full and long, and I experience each second. Among other things, I read every word of Hume's *Treatise of Human Nature* and *Lanark*, a novel I loathe. One night, after months on my own, I am woken by the sound of footsteps outside my bedroom. Sitting up, I look out my window and see a full, yellow moon surrounded by a peculiar configuration of milk-white stars:

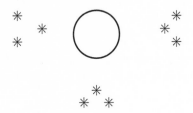

And I feel I am being told something of great importance, something only just beyond my understanding. Getting up from bed, I make my way to the door and open it. At the end of the hallway I see my mother.

—I'm so sorry, I say.

And she approaches to touch the side of my face. It

feels as though I had rubbed my cheek on oak bark. With her other hand, she takes hold of my penis, and I am as alarmed by the abrasion as by the act itself. It is like being masturbated with steel wool. There is the sound of women whispering. I am excited and humiliated, and when I nocturnally emit I smell the baby powder the women use to keep their chests dry.

This dream also stopped after my mother's death.

I suppose these dreams were the expressions of desires or fears or whatnot. I would like to say: "I understand these things. They mean . . ." But they mean nothing to me now, and I'm not sure they ever did. They seem nothing more than a hodgepodge of images that passed before me, repeatedly, and then desisted. (Am I obstinate to go on believing I will be fully recovered only when these images hold no mystery for me? Were they ever anything but mysterious? And how am I to know, now, if they are mysterious in the old way?)

Later, when Dr. Pascal had been with me for a week, I read my mother's letters. One of them reminded me of these things:

Dear Anna,

I'm sorry to say I'm not at all well. There is the house and there is the sickness and between them I feel wretched. Still, I'm not so bad that I can't get around. I manage to do my business quite well, thank you, without, need I say it, the help of that thing who calls himself my son. My only comfort, aside from your beautiful records, is knowing the poor boy will die without me, though he doesn't know it. He'll certainly die of remorse, if there is a God!

I'm afraid I'm having awful dreams again. I'll spare you the details. I'm sure I don't know what they mean or where they come from. I don't mind the old dreams, where if you saw this or that it had to do with something, but these are just a damned nuisance. Well, just a few details. The other night I dreamed we were back in Sandy Hill. You remember how it used to be. You had just married Tom N'kotu, of all people, and we were walking, you and I, in Strathcona, by the rapids. Then the sky turned red, and the clouds caught fire, and we heard someone's child had just drowned. A strange man, thin as a rake and bald as marble, approached us. He begged us for money for his experiments. I won't go into details, but it was all very frightening, and it upset me the whole day.

I can't tell you how much I appreciate the records you sent. The *Tosca* is so beautiful, I play it every day. And the *Sonnambula*, even though the tenor is pathetic, at least has Callas. I don't play it so often, but I love you for it.

Love,
Maddy

3. DR. ENRICO PASCAL

I had lived alone for months when Dr. Pascal rang the doorbell. It was a Wednesday in April. I remember it down to the last detail. First, it was early and I was still asleep. I don't usually hear the doorbell from the basement, but this morning I did, as though it were ringing beneath my pillow. The sun was up, but its light had yet to reach my bed, and though I resigned myself to getting out of bed, I decided to punish whoever it was at the door.

I turned on the radio. (It was Schumann.) Then I showered (there was no soap and the water was so hot my skin began to crack as soon as I dried myself so I had to rub my knees and elbows with baby oil). Then I ate breakfast (ham and Red River cereal). This took me half an hour, during which the doorbell was a constant irritation. It was only through force of will that I managed to ignore the buzzing and the knocking until I had wiped a blotch of cereal from my chest and put on my clothes for the day (black pants and green shirt, blue caleçons, and black socks).

—You took your time, not that I blame you, good morning, though I myself would have taken less, Dr. Enrico Pascal, busy busy busy . . .

—You woke me, I said.

—Yes, said Dr. Pascal. I can't think of a quote for morning just now, except for the early worm, which seems apposite . . . Phoebus 'gins arise, also. Your hand, let's shake on it. I need a place and you've got one. If the rent's appropriate, Phoebus can rise his ass off with me in one of your bedrooms.

—You want to rent the house?

—If my shnuts ain't on the line I do.

—There's a lot of space here. Do you have a family?

—You have a preference for fornicators?

—I prefer those who have issue to show for it, I said. That stopped him.

—You're a man of intellect, he said. I'm a man of science, myself. I need room for my work. If you could see your way to renting me the place, I'd be grateful . . . How much are you asking?

—Thousand dollars a month.

—I'll give you two . . . to make up for the lack of progeny.

Dr. Pascal had a peculiar voice. During this exchange, it went through all the registers: from high and staccato to low and smooth, from ululation to prostration. I judged it to be a professional eccentricity with which, for two thousand dollars a month, I could live.

—Come in and see the house, I said.

I led him through that part of the house he would occupy, making it clear that I would expect privacy, that two thousand dollars a month gave him dominion of the upper floors only.

—Shame about the carpet, he said.

—Most people like carpet.

—Most people aren't scientists. There's little enough electricity involved, but I use gouts of corrosive chemicals. Chemicals to turn this rug into a stinking morass faster than you could cut the testicles from a cadaver's scrotum, as we said at the alma mater . . . Nothing a little plastic wouldn't save, though.

—You're a doctor, then?

—I was last time I looked.

—A medical doctor?

—A medical doctor. Now, that's your share of Q and A. Rent me the place and we'll get on like Rome under Nero, n'est-ce pas?

Dr. Pascal's paraphernalia came the following day in two half-ton trucks. It was brought in by four or five men who worked like zombies. I kept out of the way. I heard his shouted commands at breakfast and lunch only. By evening, all was quiet, all was in order.

—No plastic, he said as he led me through his rooms. I put my own carpet down over yours.

Which made the floors elastic and thick.

Dr. Pascal's carpeting was dull brown, institutional. The rooms themselves, save my mother's, in which he had put his books and a narrow, unmattressed cot, were taken over by metal tables and cabinets. On the tables were a bewildering number of phials, beakers, alembics, torches, plastic bags of powders of every color, and jars of liquids in some of which were specimens of a variety of small animals: worms, frogs, pig fetuses, birds, rats, mice, kittens, fish, and wolverines. In my younger sister's room, in a large tank of formaldehyde, was a greyhound that had been shaved hairless.

—I'm proud of this, he said.

When he put a wire into the solution the dog began to move its legs back and forth as though it were swimming.

The only room not given over to his paraphernalia

was the living room. It had been left uncarpeted. Instead, hundreds of short pieces of two-by-four had been laid side by side and end to end so that you could no longer see the floor.

—Mark my words, boy. This is where it all begins.

—What is it?

—If you help me out, say Saturday, you'll see. It'll take time before it's done, but I'll pay, of course. I'll disburse for your time. But it must be done soon.

I had no interest in any of it. I was satisfied that he had not permanently marred the house, and I would have been happy to leave him to his business, but the money tempted me and I agreed to help him. (What kind of a man says yes without conviction?)

That Saturday evening, Dr. Pascal accosted me as I came into the house through my own entrance, downstairs.

—What are you doing here? I asked.

—A fuss about that? Kicking up his heels on his high horse when I have the lucre? It's the week's end. We have to start right away.

He was still a stranger to me, so I treated him with deference. I took off my jacket and followed him to the living room.

—Grab some epoxy, he said.

I find it hard to describe my surprise, and then the hours of boredom that followed it, as we set about gluing staples to the pieces of wood on the floor. Each staple had to be glued upright to the pencil marks

Dr. Pascal had made on the wood. The staples, in groups of two, were roughly one centimeter apart, with two centimeters separating the clusters. He had finished dozens of pieces himself, and these looked as though they had grown silver bristles.

—Fifty bucks a board, he said.

Under the circumstances, I couldn't think of anything to ask. I finished twenty-five of them.

—Let's just test those, he said.

And from a specimen bottle he took a housefly. Carefully, he put the fly between two staples and closed the ends of the staples in so the insect was firmly gripped by the head, or eyes, and thorax, just beneath its wings.

—A moment, he said.

And, after a while, the fly, which I had thought dead, began to hum.

—Perfect, he said. I make that 1,250 dollars.

Silence.

—Like this they can still feed, he said.

The living room was twenty feet by twenty, or thereabouts. With each piece of wood being twelve inches long, there were 1,200 of them in all.

—The body has to be cared for, he said.

And a week later there were thousands of flies in their harnesses on the living-room floor.

4. Fresh Air

I was not really interested in Dr. Pascal's business, but out of politeness I asked one or two questions.

—Why are these flies on the floor?

—Want to know?

—Yes.

—I'd like, if you comprehend, to have them die at the same time, all at once, all together.

He had a large aluminium tin with the word "sugar" written on it in Gothic script. From the tin he took handfuls of crystal and dispersed them in the living room, as though it were grain for chickens.

—You want to kill them? I asked.

—Not in the least! I want them to give up the ghost in concert, as one, don't you know.

He looked up at me.

—Yes, you *should* know. You should know . . . I believe, my boy, it's possible to separate the body from the—for lack of a more appropriate word you know— soul. This sugar is tainted, it's drugged, a neural stimulant. So far so good. The flies feed, they die, their bodies go on, and I measure the energy of their, as you say, souls . . . just one of many ideas . . .

—Their souls?

—I don't call it soul, mind you. Now, si vous permettez . . . I'll tell you all about it in a day or two.

—No need, I said. I don't have a scientific mind.

—Of course you don't, but you have a mind.

Silence.

—Good night, he said.

· · ·

This particular conversation brought back the conundrums that used to frighten me as a child, the business of the soul I mean. For instance, if a rat were to eat a consecrated host, would it go to Heaven? (How many rats have eaten the body of Christ?) Are their souls carnivorous, or psychovorous, without cheese? (I felt pity for the angels whom I imagined fluttering their wings in revulsion. It also occurred to me that a rat's nature might change in Heaven, that there was perhaps a celestial element to "ratness." I must have been subtle as a child, but did I really believe?) And now there was the business of the flies. (Did I believe?)

I began to avoid Dr. Pascal, gently. But, true to his word, he knocked at my door a few nights later and invited me to supper.

—I will tell all, he said.

Now, let me resume: My mother died. I lived in an empty house. I rented the top of the house to a man named Pascal. He began to use the house for his experiments. When some of the experiments were over, he invited me to dinner.

Where, in these incidents, was there warning? I had had dreams. My mother had had dreams. But what are dreams? No, I should have been more alert. I should have thought: First the flies, and then what?

And then Dr. Pascal put his bit of poison in my food, or my coffee, or whatever was at hand.

. . .

My first night was peculiar:

Dr. Pascal's dinner made me sleepy, but not so that I was conscious of being drugged. Tired: my body was heavy as wet sand, but I took this for postprandial fatigue.

—So, you see? A complete success, said Dr. Pascal. But, I must be boring you with the details, n'est-ce pas?

—Yes.

I went downstairs, slowly, and fell into bed. The light in the bedroom was still on, and in trying to get up, I felt my legs come up out of my body. I had my first, rather late, inkling that something was wrong. I saw Dr. Pascal's face above mine. He said:

—Entre o sono e o sohno, entre mim e o que em mim, E o quem eu me suponho, Corre um rio sem fim . . .

Or sounds to that effect. And part of me fell asleep for the last time.

And I woke almost immediately. I woke to the sounds of a million voices and a body in bed beside me. Thinking it to be Dr. Pascal, misinterpreting his motives for putting me under, I jumped up and recognized my own poor body.

How homely I was. I was thirty-five years old, five feet and seven inches tall (long), one hundred and fifty pounds. Of course, I had realized some time before that I was a negro, but this "niggerness" still surprised me. My hair was like a cone of wool. My mouth hung open and the side of my face was white with spittle. My eyes were open, and I was breathing. (I mean my chest rose and fell as I've seen other chests do.) My body was on its side, turned away from the wall, looking at me, or toward me, seeing nothing.

You might think my first feeling would be panic, but I was calm. (I am speaking, now, for both of us.) I was surprised, of course, but only mildly, and aside from the loathing I felt for my body, I was at ease. As I mentioned, I could hear the sounds of millions of voices, not whispering, but speaking softly, as though I were in a million confessionals.

Dr. Pascal came into the room without ceremony. He passed between my two selves, and I had the odd experience of seeing him, briefly, from both sides. In his hand he had a piece of paper on which was typed:

Ottawa

a) Lowertown

b) Sandy Hill

c) Centre Town

d) Lebreton Flats

e) Mechanicsville

f) Hintonburg	l) Carlingwood
g) Glebe	m) Mooney's Bay
h) Ottawa East	n) Woodroffe
i) Ottawa South	o) Manor Park
j) Sheffield Glen	p) Brittania
k) Vincent Alexander Park	q) Hampton Park

r) Lincoln Heights   w) Elmvale Acres
s) Castle Heights   x) Urbandale
t) Riverside Park   y) Hawthorne Meadow
u) Rideau Gardens   z) Billings Bridge
v) Manor Park

1. Home

—A little experiment, he said. Here's what we'll do . . .

He took out from his pocket a roll of narrow masking tape, and on my brow he taped the letters:

FIGLZ

—Up an' at 'em, he said.

I heard his voice quite clearly, but after a delay. I saw his lips move without hearing a sound. Then I heard his voice, when his lips had stopped moving. My body got up from the bed and began to walk about briskly. It walked through the house, and once outside, I climbed on my own shoulders in order to keep up.

This was the most exhilarating walk I have ever taken, if that is the way to describe it. I didn't actually feel the night air, but I sensed it. The sky was a hard, deep black, and flatter than I have ever seen it. Each of the stars was blue and brilliant as sparks from a forge. I felt I was in danger of dispersing, but for the palms of the trees that protected me as though I were a small light.

The entire city was different. The lights were brighter, the shadows darker. The Rideau was black and smooth as noxious gelatin. The pavement was gray, porous as bread.

We walked to Gladstone and Sherbrooke
>to Sunnyside and Bank
>to Lyon and Third
>to Merivale and Shillington
>to Billings Bridge Plaza

But what was, at first, an ecstatic pilgrimage became, as we moved away from Bank and Riverside, something of a threat to my existence. By Merivale and Shillington, I was terrified. I felt as though my heart were being wrung out and rubbed against splintered wood. The voices I heard grew louder and more hostile. I was on the point of falling from my own shoulders when we turned back to Billings Bridge. The voices dimmed, the pain subsided with each step we made back, and in this way I came to understand that, in this state, I could not live comfortably far from my own home.

Waiting for us when we reached the Plaza, Dr. Pascal tore the strips of masking tape from my forehead and, putting his arm in mine, led us back to the house.

5. MENS SANA IN CORPORE SANO

What exactly did Dr. Pascal want with my body? He seemed unconcerned that I was "about" in another form. And, though he had all manner of equipment, he made no effort to communicate with me, with either of us.

I should have felt betrayed or angry, but I felt nothing like it. I felt longing for my body at the same time as my loathing for my physical self increased. (This seems confusing to me now, but it was as though I felt love for a large rat.) My brown eyes disgusted me. My flat nose was horrifying. My ears seemed like coils of abandoned snake skin. As for the rest, the less said, et cetera.

It surprised me to think of my body in these terms. I had had my minor revulsions before, certainly, but nothing so distinct. I tried to recall the "pleasures of the body," but they were remarkably few: I had once swum in deep, clear water and then lay down in the sun, on rocky sand that smelled of the plantains, milkweed, and thistles in the field beside the quarry ... Too little to inspire nostalgia, that. And, besides, it disturbed me when my body followed me through the house.

Feeling as I did, I couldn't help my little cruelties: I went from the top of the house to the basement, relentlessly, until my body collapsed in its efforts to keep up, opening and closing its mouth, shuddering like a dying fish. I went slowly before it, so it could keep up, and then popped through a wall into which it would thump. (I gave myself quite a few bloody noses this way.) I had, as I mentioned, ordered the house alphabetically, and trusting that it remembered the significance of each room, I said:

. . .

spare bedroom
family room
walk-in closet

And then:

boiler room
father's office
foyer
walk-in closet

And then watched as understanding dawned, and my body cried. (I mean *I* cried; *I* broke my nose; *I* panted for breath. *I* was jilted.)

We were at an impasse that seemed to last forever. (I judged the passing of time by the number of excursions my body made into the city. I no longer went with it. Dr. Pascal sent it out; it executed its trajectory and then returned. I no longer "saw" through my eyes, but I could still "see," and I got on well without my senses. I had memory, but I lost interest in remembering the moments of my previous life. I remembered the first seven trips my body made into the city after FIGLZ, though:

1. diewcoeu
2. eltiraso
3. stalnord
4. leswrele

5. asdespri
6. rfaltale
7. listsien

And I tried to tease some sense out of these letters. Having lived in Ottawa for so long without really seeing it, I could not attach any specific meanings to Lebreton Flats (d) or Ottawa South (i), Mechanicsville (e) or Elmvale Acres (w). They were not particularly interesting parts of town (for me), and their relation escaped me completely. I thought I could make out words here and there. For instance, in the first string was "dieu," in the second "lira," or "tira," and in the third "sa," "ta," or "nord," et cetera. I managed to pick out: *dieu tira nord les dés fatal(s),* but by then I had begun to lose command of my languages, and though I knew these were words, I couldn't make any sense of them. My soul was losing touch with time and the world.)

And then, after a time, I began to feel the pull of my body. I felt an unwelcome and irresistible call back. I can't say where this call came from, but finally, I began to reinsert myself. That is, I consciously occupied the same space my body did.

Naturally, my body and I were not immediately comfortable. There was too much light. My senses produced only one impression: I heard brightness; I felt brightness; I tasted brightness; I was permeated by light. And, at first, I could not stand this for more than a little at a time. But each day I went in for longer and longer until, on the first of June, I could not get back out.

Of all that had happened to me since April, these

first days in June were the most unpleasant. There was the light, which only gradually separated into my senses. There was the air about me and my lungs shuddering like a broken water pump. I heard cars and birds and voices from outside the house. I could tell night from day, and I saw my body from that ridiculous perspective we assume to be normal. The inside of my mouth tasted like I had bitten a centipede.

When Dr. Pascal came to put his letters on my forehead that evening, I held him off and tried to curse him. I made sounds like a foghorn. He went to get a stick.

I moved out of the way as best I could, but I was not agile. I kept my arms up, but he hit my knuckles. He held the stick out before me until I took hold of it, awkwardly, with both hands. He tried to speak to me, but what I heard was a string of sounds. (I presume he spoke English. It sounded like a dog's bark.) He left me holding the stick and went off to get a piece of bristol board on which he had written:

WELCOME BACK
JE TE SOUHAITE LA BIENVENUE

I didn't understand this any better than I had his spoken noise.

The first emotion I felt that day was one of extreme hatred for Dr. Pascal coupled with the frustration of being unable to direct my body to throttle him. Not only had I lost my language(s), the one(s) I used to communicate, but I had also lost the language I used to speak with my body, the one my body used to speak to me.

I have a tendency to speak of my (so-called) mind as "I," but that's not exactly what I felt. My body was "I" as well. The constant unfolding of images, words, and desires that I take to be consciousness was, for the first few days, bifurcate. I mean, it was as though I were in a movie theater and there were two screens instead of one. On the first: the needs and impulses of my body. On the second: the noises and images of my mind. I myself, neither one nor the other, had to choose between the two. If I paid too much attention to my mind, I was incontinent or cataleptic. If I paid attention to my body, I could not think what to do. I could react instinctively, of course, but it was a full week before I could, for instance, listen and walk at the same time. Naturally, during this time I was vulnerable to Dr. Pascal's predation, so I tried to eat, sleep, and drink as little as possible.

Contrary to my expectations, Dr. Pascal did not try to drug me. Perhaps he hadn't expected I would return. Perhaps my aggression surprised him. Whatever the reason, he seemed content to observe, to keep his distance. He took notes on my behavior, which he put down in a blue duo-tang, and hundreds of photographs of me as I stood still or tried to walk away.

After a week I was able to drink water from a tap, eat handfuls of stale bread, open cans of pork and beans. I could voice my displeasure. I could wipe the sweat from my forehead. The only thing that didn't work was sleep. I would lock myself in my room, push my bed up against the door so Dr. Pascal couldn't enter, but though my body relaxed, my mind would not. I no longer dreamed.

(I began this narrative with my dreams, with the only two I remember, because they are the last of their species. I still rummage through them for some idea of who I was before my crisis. I ruminate on the type of man who dreams of headless assailants, of sex with his mother, and so on.)

6. JOUAL

Every morning, after my first week back, Dr. Pascal would point to an object with a stick and he would say, for instance:

—What is it? It's a cup. A cup. What is it?

And if I answered cup, and if it really were a cup, he would nod his head and proceed. If I didn't answer, or if I gave the wrong answer, he would strike me.

—What is it?

—Cup.

—Full sentence: it is a cup.

—It is a cup.

—Qu'est-ce que c'est? C'est une tasse. Qu'est-ce que c'est?

—Une tasse.

—Une phrase: ceci est une tasse.

—Cela est une tasse.

He was aggressively Berlitz, but I have a gift for language so I easily avoided the stick. (I suspected these lessons were a continuation of his experiments on another plane, but I needed them. So I didn't murder him.)

In this way, Dr. Pascal became something of a father to me. It is a complicated situation. I can't live without his money, his lessons, his time. And, though I won't eat anything he prepares, or help him with his experiments, I have begun to accept him. I hate him, but for all my hatred I can't throw him off. (Besides, he's the only one who understands me as I am now.) Certainly, when I have finally deciphered my dreams and recovered my previous way of thinking, I will get rid of him . . .

—Le mot anglais pour "joual"?
—Horse.

My Anabasis

There's a restlessness that sometimes pushes me out. I don't know where it comes from or what purpose it serves, but it's there behind most of the things I do. For instance,

1. Leaving

I was in Ottawa and things weren't going well. I was unhappy and I knew it, and once I'm in the grip of a real depression the only thing that helps is travel.

It sounds simple, doesn't it? You pack your bags and go. But first you need a viable destination. That's what makes it complicated. If I'm in Ottawa and I go to Carleton Place, what are my chances for Happiness? Nil. Same with Toronto, Sudbury, Windsor, or London. Even at my worst I need a proper destination.

Then, on January 11th, my wife received a letter meant for someone else. It read:

Dear Andrée,

I love you. I dream of you nightly. In my dreams I can smell your long, blonde hair. I caress your breasts and touch your dark nipples with my tongue. I dream of you as you were last summer. Do you remember, my love, how we lay on your bed? You were sweet as cough syrup. I dream of you like that.

Please, my love, come back to Ottawa. We can stay at the Venture. I'll give you everything. I promise.

All my love,
André

The letter was addressed to:

Andrée Alexis
160 Percy Street
Ottawa, Ontario

And the return address, printed on the back of the envelope, was:

André Alexis
12 Newcastle Drive
Ottawa, New York
10057

Now, Andrée and I *do* live at 160 Percy, but she is a redhead and her nipples are not unusually dark.

Moreover, I had her assurance that she'd never been to Ottawa, New York. So, Mr. Alexis had not tasted *my* wife.

The strange thing was that I too had lived at 12 Newcastle Drive, but in Ottawa, Ontario. Think how rare it is to receive a letter at your current address from someone at your previous. In the mood I was in, the coincidence was enough to set me off.

The next day, I took most of my money from our joint account, wrote a letter to my wife explaining my need to travel, packed a suitcase full of shoes and socks, and got on the train for New York.

2. SKIRMISH

The train at night is usually filled with youths traveling without parental guidance. They're up all night, drinking from wineskins filled with Lemon Gin, shouting, arguing, laughing out loud. This trip was different. There were kids all over the place, but I had a seat by a window, and I was with three adults.

Facing me was a middle-aged man in a tweed jacket and a white turtleneck. His hair was red; his eyes an odd shade of green. To his left was a woman in a tweed jacket with matching skirt. Her hair was long and brown; her nose aquiline, with flared nostrils. She had a wide face. Her eyes were round and her mouth extremely small. Facing her, to my immediate right, was a man in his thirties. His hair was dark and extremely short. His thick-rimmed glasses seemed to rest on his cheekbones, so small was his nose, and he was casually dressed.

As the train left the station, the couple in tweed began to relax. They exchanged a few words, in their American accent, and then, after a while, the man turned to me and said:

—Quite a country you people have here.

—Yes, it's beautiful, I said.

—It's the first time we've been here, he continued, and we like it so much we're coming back, eh, darling?

The woman turned to me and smiled. It didn't seem possible for her to speak with such a small mouth, but she said:

—I sure hope so . . .

—By the way, I'm André and this is my wife Andrée.

—Pleased to meet you, I said.

—We're from New York. We're just up on vacation, and I'm glad we picked Ottawa instead of Toronto, like we were going to . . . It sure is beautiful, if you don't mind the cold. Of course, we get our share of cold in New York, but not like you people up here . . . Who's your friend there?

He turned to the man beside me and smiled.

—Je ne parle pas l'anglais, my neighbor said.

—Il vous demande votre nom, I said.

—Dites-lui qu'il peut me sucer le noeud, maudit américain impérialiste. J'ai pas oublié le Vietnam, moi.

—What did he say?

—He said you were a damned American imperialist, and you can suck his privates because he hasn't forgotten Vietnam.

Mr. Alexis stopped talking. He tilted his head and looked to my neighbor, who smiled courteously.

—Did he really say all that? he said.

—Yes, I said. I'm afraid so.

Mr. and Mrs. Alexis looked at each other and began to laugh.

—Well, said Mr. Alexis, you people have a strange way of talking to visitors. Does he want to fight right here or does he want to step into the aisle?

—Voulez-vous vous battre ici ou dans le couloir? I asked.

—Comment ça "me battre"? he said. Je suis pas violent, moi. J'ai dis la vérité, un point c'est tout. S'il veut se battre avec quelqu'un c'est son problème. Qu'il aille se faire enculer.

—What did he say?

—He said he doesn't want to fight. If you want to fight that's your problem, and you can go get fucked.

Mr. Alexis turned and looked me in the eye.

—Are you making this up?

—I don't make things up, I said. I haven't got a creative bone in my body . . .

At that moment, the Frenchman smiled and said in his best English:

—I hope you enjoy your trip, hein.

—What do you mean? asked Mr. Alexis.

—I love America, my neighbor answered. I love America.

Mr. Alexis turned to me and said:

—You nasty son of a bitch. He didn't say any of that stuff you said.

The small-mouthed wife said:

—Leave it alone, André. It isn't worth the trouble. He's just crazy's his problem.

All three of them were looking at me. Mr. Alexis's temples were throbbing. His wife was contemptuous. The Frenchman was amused.

—J't'ai bien eu, hein connard? Qui t'a dit que je voulais un traducteur? Occupe-toi de tes oignons . . . okay?

He sat back in his seat, smiling graciously at the Americans.

—I love America, he repeated.

The problem with me is that I don't know how to deal with these things when they happen. I felt humiliated, but I didn't know what to do. I wanted to tear the little frog's head off, but instead I sat still and turned my head away from the three of them.

Mr. Alexis said:

—You are some son of a bitch.

Then he sat back. His wife took a book from her purse and started to read. The Frenchman took off his coat, pulled a tattered *Evénement de Jeudi* from its inside pocket, and sat back. From then until we crossed the American border, none of us spoke.

Just after the border crossing, my neighbor began a conversation with the Americans.

—Is it New York?

—Yeah, said Mr. Alexis. We live in New York City.

—A nice city, non?

—If you like big cities. I'm from the country myself. Where you from?

—Where you from? Qu'est-ce que ça veut dire "where you from"?

They turned to me. I could see their faces reflected in the window. Naturally, I didn't say a word.

—Hé, couillon, qu'est-ce que ça veut dire "where you from"?

—You Canadian? Mr. Alexis asked.

—Non, non . . . Français. French. Paris.

—He's from Paris, dear, said Mrs. Alexis.

—You from Paris?

—Ah oui, said my neighbor. From Paris.

—That's a beautiful city, said Mrs. Alexis. We were there two years ago.

The three of them began to talk about Paris and New York. They were getting along. That's what made me angry. So, when the porter came by with hot coffee, it was all I could do to ask politely for coffee and a doughnut.

The coffee was in one of those silver cylinders with a spigot near the bottom and, going up the side, a graduated glass tube that shows you how much coffee is left. When the porter pulled the black plastic regulator forward, a cloud of steam escaped and the coffee ran into my foam cup.

—There you go. That'll be two fifty.

He handed me the coffee and a square plastic envelope in which I could see my greasy sugared doughnut. I leaned forward, and as if by accident, I threw the hot coffee in the Frenchman's face.

The effect was immediate. The man began to wail and he tried to hold his face. Then, there was movement all around me. I said:

—Oh, I'm sorry . . .

Mr. Alexis pushed me back.

—You careless idiot, he said.

Mrs. Alexis cooed sympathetically, and the porter, not knowing what to do, came back to help the Frenchman stand up. My neighbor's face was red; the skin had already begun to blister. He let out soft little cries of alarm. His glasses had fallen to the floor. I crushed them beneath my feet. The frames flew apart and the lenses cracked.

—Oh, I'm sorry, I said.

But no one was listening to me. Mr. Alexis had gotten up to follow the Frenchman and the porter down the aisle. Mrs. Alexis got up to get a better look at the action. Everyone else in the car did the same. So I pushed what was left of his glasses beneath the Frenchman's seat, and I followed the procession behind the porter, to show my concern for the victim.

At the first-aid station, which was actually the porter's enclave at the end of the car, they had managed to find a doctor. The doctor had his hand in a black box full of gauze, bandages, and ointments. The Frenchman was babbling in French. No, actually, he wasn't babbling. He was saying:

—Il l'a fait exprès. Il l'a fait exprès. Où sont mes lunettes? J'vois rien sans mes lunettes. Il l'a fait exprès . . .

—Tes lunettes sont en mille morceaux, I said.

—You speak French? asked the doctor.

—A little, I answered.

—There's some ointment here and some bandages. I'm going to have to wrap his face. He's pretty badly burned. Ask him if he's allergic to anything.

—Es-tu allergique à quelque chose?

—Oui, he answered. Je ne peux pas prendre la pénicilline.

—I got that, the doctor said. He can't take penicillin, right?

—That's right, I said.

—Tell him not to worry. There's no penicillin in this ointment, but he's got to sit still so we can put it on.

—Malheureusement, I said, ils n'ont que de la pénicilline. Calme-toi . . .

At this the Frenchman really began to struggle.

—Non, non, he said, ça me tuera. J'suis allergique. It kill me! It kill me!

—He says the pain is killing him.

The Frenchman struggled as if his life depended on it, and he did quite well for a man in pain. They had to call several porters to hold him down, to keep him still, to spread the ointment on his face. I left the scene as he began to kick out. I would have stayed, but the ointment reminded me of a burn I'd suffered as a child. It recalled the way my shirt had stuck to my skin, the sound of the doctors' voices, and the smell of the hospital.

I was so gratified at seeing the Frenchman suffer, I didn't notice Mr. Alexis had followed me back to the bay. As I sat down, he tapped me on the shoulder and said:

—You did that on purpose, didn't you?

He was taunting me, so I answered in the most litigious voice I could muster:

—I don't know what you're talking about, but I know a good lawyer, and I'll sue you if you ever say that in public again. You know what litigation is, don't you?

He stood there with his mouth open. Being American, he knew all about litigation. (It's a lovely word. It always reminded me of "ligament," and as a child I imagined the men in court snipping the Achilles tendons of the guilty.) He snorted derisively, but he shut up.

The rest of the trip to New York was uneventful. I looked out the window at the stars and, when we passed through cloudless regions, the moonlit farms, the sharp edges of small towns.

When the Frenchman was brought back to his seat, held up by two large, unhappy porters, he was under sedation. His face was swaddled in sticky yellow gauze and he stank of balm. Only his eyes, ears, and the top of his head were left uncovered. He slumped forward in his seat.

—Bad posture, I said.

I was only trying to lighten the atmosphere, but Mr. and Mrs. Alexis were in no mood for talk. The small-mouthed bitch was still immersed in *The Mountain and the Valley*, and her cowardly husband was doing his best to ignore me.

3. Traveling Alone

Unfortunately, the beginning of a trip casts its shadow forward. It sets the mood.

From the moment I stepped into Grand Central Station, I began to notice people with bandages. The man at the kiosk where I bought my map of New York State had his right hand in a sling. The driver of the bus that took me to Ottawa had two of the fingers on his right hand bound to a wooden splint. And the woman who sat beside me on the bus had a Band-Aid over her left eyebrow. Everywhere I turned there were echoes of the Frenchman. It didn't help my disposition.

The day after my train ride, I left New York City for Ottawa, New York. The bus backed out of the terminal and wound through the city: from Elgin to Rideau, from Rideau to Bank, and from Bank to Somerset, past the harbor and the Statue of Liberty.

As soon as we got out of the city, I fell asleep, and for a while:

I was alone on a country road. There were farmyards, and fence posts. The fence posts were unusual. On top of each one there was my head: my head, eyes open, every four feet or so. I got off the bus in the middle of nowhere and discovered that all the heads were speaking at once. The countryside sounded like a terminal, and the fields went on forever. One of the heads spoke.

—*Hey you! C'mere, lemme look at you. You been walking much? Hard on the soles? Jeez, I haven't had a good conversation in ages . . . Say, get closer, will ya. I haven't had any human contact in so long . . .*

But I walked away along the narrow road, listening to the wolf whistles, jeers, and curses of every head I passed.

4. OTTAWA

I stepped down into the archetypal American city. It looked as it had looked on countless television shows, and it was much as I'd imagined it from magazines and novels. (It was a little cleaner than I'd expected, but that didn't throw me.)

The streets were manageable. Two of the main roads were four lanes wide; the rest were comfortably two-laned. The wider streets were Laurier, which ran north-south, and Somerset, which was east-west. It was easy to get around and difficult to get lost. I hate that in a city. After hours of walking about, I felt as though I'd lived in the place forever.

The Alexises' house at 12 Newcastle was as I'd expected: a red-bricked, two-storied, chimneyed abode whose window frames were painted white, and in one of whose windows was a white flower box from which dry brown vines tumbled. In a window on the second floor, I could see a young woman with a white babushka wrapped around her head. She stopped to wipe her brow and then went on with what looked like vacuuming, though it could have been sweeping, or mime, for all I could see.

It was cold outside, so I rang the doorbell.

—Yes?

An older woman stood on her side of the screen door, and for an awful moment I thought she was André's wife.

—Does André Alexis live here? I asked.

—Certainly, she said. You can see it on the mailbox.

—Is he home?

—No.

She stood there staring at me, waiting for the next question. It was like an intelligence test.

—Do you know when he'll be back? I said.

—No.

Then, from somewhere inside the house, a woman's voice:

—Who is it, Mother?

—I don't know.

—A friend of André's, I said.

—A friend of André's, said the old lady.

Then the young woman I'd seen in the window was with us, her hand on her mother's shoulder, smiling faintly through the screen door.

She looked corn-fed and healthy. Her eyes were big,

round, and green. She had freckles across the bridge of her nose. Her hair, which fell from the babushka in strands, was red. She was wearing a shirt several sizes too big for her and I could see the plain white brassiere beneath it, and the outlines of her body. She had perspired, so the shirt clung to her skin here and there.

—My name's André Alexis, I said. Has André ever mentioned me?

—Not that I can recall, she said.

—Oh, that's just like him. I'll come back when he's home. Nice to have met you . . .

I didn't move, but the old lady began to push the door closed.

—Just a minute. Won't you come inside a moment? I'll call my husband at work; let him know you're here.

The old woman now had to pull the door open. She stood there, panting slightly, looking at me like I was a thief. I wasn't even tempted to make conversation.

—He's right here, would you like to speak to him?

André's wife called me to the telephone and put the warm receiver in my hand.

—Hello? Who is this? André asked.

—It's André. André Alexis.

—Do I know you?

—I'm fine, fine. I was just talking to Andrée. I live with her on Percy Street. I got your last letter where you mentioned our cough syrup, so I thought I'd visit.

I was looking at his wife when I said this. She brushed the hair from her eyes.

—Who is this? André said.

—You've got a lovely wife, I said. Why didn't you tell her about me?

—What are you talking about? Are you talking about Andrée? How do you know about her?

—Hey, there'll be lots of time to talk about that when you get home. I'll pass you back to your wife.

I cut him off and gave the warm receiver back to his wife.

—Hi, Ange, she said.

And rubbed first one palm and then the next on her moist shirt. She listened, then she said:

—Bye, Ange.

And made a kissing sound, like balloons being rubbed, and hung up.

—He'll be home at six. Mother, you can close the door now . . . You can close the door. Mr. Alexis will be staying.

To me, she said:

—So . . . I'm Andrée, and this is my mother, Andrée. I'm pleased to meet you. Come in and sit down . . . Tell us how you know André . . .

5. TRUE LOVE

We sat in the living room, Andrée facing me in the baby-blue armchair, her mother beside me on the baby-blue sofa, and I invented a long, happy friendship between myself and André. Not too long, and not too happy. I placed significant gaps here and there, lapses of time during which André and I had not spoken, to explain why he mightn't have mentioned me, to give me something to be contrite about.

The old woman sat quietly beside me, her mottled hands resting nervously in her lap. She was wearing a light-green dress, a white sweater, thick stockings, and fluffy white slippers. I could tell she was in a medical predicament because, at regular intervals, she would fart, silently but obviously, so that a rank smell came from her direction every few minutes and enveloped me. (I didn't think so at the time, but I now believe this was Andrée's way of showing her distrust. Had she really trusted me, she would have put me somewhere out of the line of her mother's fire.)

When I had finished my side of the story, Andrée told me hers: They had met between Ottawa, Kentucky, and Ottawa, New York, on a bus, of all places. She had recently sprained her ankle, and André insisted she put her foot on his footrest. He was reading a novel. What was it? Oh yes, *The Mountain and the Valley*. They'd struck up a conversation, and then he did something unexpectedly kind: he read to her from his book.

—". . . it was night and cold and the lights of the city were haloed. I could smell the ocean as I walked the streets . . ."

And she'd fallen asleep, her head against the cool window, his voice fading. The next thing she knew, they were being woken by the bus driver. It was Albany, and they could go no farther because of the storm, so they decided to spend the night in the same hotel . . . That night they talked and talked, they had so much in common, and André fell asleep on her floor, his mouth open on the carpet, his hair gray with dust balls . . . And from that night: "We've been apart only when he goes on his business trips . . . Would you like some coffee?"

You could see she was in love. She blushed at the memory of their first night, and I thought to myself: How little it takes! A man tells her to put her feet up, reads to her from a Canadian novel, then passes out on the floor of her hotel room. Is *that* what it takes to inspire love? It made me unbearably angry. And, seeing the enraptured look on her face, I felt it would be best if I destroyed everything: their home, their feelings for each other, their daily lives . . .

—That's a very touching story, I said.

She said:

—I guess I better finish my housework. If you'd like to freshen up, there's a cot in the room at the end of the hall. You could lie down for a while . . .

I got up quickly.

—Thank you.

It was a relief to get away from the old lady.

The room at the end of the hall was narrow and cold. There was just space for the cot and a chest of drawers and not much else. Still, it was the kind of room I like: it was white, recently painted, with a single window. There was no confusion and little dirt. The more a room is a mausoleum, the better I sleep.

I had a lot to think about. What was I to do about André Alexis? What was fitting punishment for his loutish behavior? Clearly, he didn't deserve his wife's love. So, the first step, after I'd convinced him to let me stay, was to alienate her affections. I would have to seduce his wife, but what was the best way to perform that service? She was obviously romantic, and she did adore her husband. (It was almost religious the way she glowed at the memory of their first night.) Did she like to talk, or was it physical affection she wanted? Should I nuzzle her ears as we squeezed by each other going in and out of doors? Did she like illicit contact? Should I touch her breasts or her arm or her bottom? How much pressure in the touch? Or was she strictly cerebral? It had been ages since I'd read *The Mountain and the Valley*, but I remembered the story: an emotionally disturbed boy becomes an unstable adult who, while running away from himself, causes the death of an innocent woman and her mother. Typical Canadian fare. Not very promising as a guide to sexual preference. Then again, maybe she enjoyed the direct approach, a declaration of erotic madness, say, or an indecent proposal made while I had an erection . . . I wondered if my morning erection would serve the purpose, and then I wondered if there were some way to prolong it until afternoon . . . Then there was her mother. Could I get on Andrée's good side by flattering her mother? With these questions in mind, I fell asleep.

I woke up at six o'clock to the sound of the front door closing. It sounded masculine: the paterfamilias returning, master of all he surveys, a newspaper tucked under his arm, a briefcase in one hand, leather gloves in the other, ready to touch the dog, the wife, the children. It's a sound that reminds me of having my hair tousled. I sat up and found myself in a darkened room, the light from the streetlamp outside just touching the bottom of the window. It took a few minutes, but I remembered where I was, got up, and went out to meet Mr. Alexis.

He wasn't what I expected. To begin with, he was thin and a trifle effeminate. I could tell by looking at him he used cologne, so I wasn't surprised when his scent reached me. His face was narrow, but he had a large jaw. I put out my hand and said:

—Hello, André. It's been a long time . . .

I could see he wasn't about to shake with me, so I put my arms around him and gave him the college hug.

—Good to see you, man . . .

He stiffened as though he'd been splashed.

—You haven't changed a bit, I said.

His wife hovered about somewhere, smiling politely. His mother-in-law was where I'd left her. She hadn't moved in hours, it seemed.

—I've got one of your letters, I said.

And pulled out the envelope so he alone could see it:

Andrée Alexis
160 Percy Street
Ottawa, Ontario

That changed his mood. He became a little more agreeable. He said:

—Yes . . .

I said:

—Give us the old college kiss . . .

I embraced him, made the sound of a kiss, and followed that with a raspberry.

There was a moment of dead silence. Then, his wife said she was going to see to the liver and onions, and she left us to renew our peculiar acquaintance. He and I stepped into the living room, where his mother-in-law had recently farted.

—What do you want? he asked.

—Your mother-in-law . . .

—She's dirt poor.

—No. I mean she can hear us. I'm not sure you want that . . .

—She's stone deaf and senile. What do you want?

—I want to stay for a while. I don't want money. I want a bit of hospitality. That's all anybody wants, isn't it?

—Why here?

I held up the letter to Andrée.

—Because you owe me.

Mr. Alexis looked neither desperate nor guilty. He seemed to recognize the letter. It was important, but I wasn't sure why.

—Let me see the letter, he said.

—You don't need to see the letter. In fact, you're lucky I don't kick you to death and burn your house down. I came here to see what kind of man pokes another man's wife, then writes her dirty letters. I'll hang around awhile, so you can explain it to me.

I was more aggressive than I'd meant to be, but he

didn't seem to mind. He smiled. His face reddened. There was something wrong here.

—Well, I'm sorry about your wife, he said.

He frowned as his mother-in-law passed gas. He took my arm; we moved away from the old woman.

—Listen, he whispered. I didn't write that letter. Let me read it; maybe we can get to the bottom of all this . . .

I didn't believe him, but I held it up so he could read it.

—Yes, I see . . . , he whispered.

The evening meal was eaten in near silence, and it took hours. Mrs. Alexis was as agreeable as ever, but much of her time was taken up with her mother, who sat at the head of the table. Andrée cut the breaded liver into ragged pieces and put them on her mother's spoon. Mr. Alexis cut his food and deliberately smushed his portions. It looked like he was eating a liver, onion, and potato paste.

—It's been a long time, I said, to keep up my end of the charade.

No one was listening. It was then I had my first inkling something was wrong.

They were clearly speaking to each other in a language I couldn't quite understand. There was something said in a configuration of peas, or a cough. An answer was given in spittle, in the angle of a fork. My case was discussed and decided, without my having understood a word.

After supper, the four of us sat in the living room.

Andrée, her mother, and myself on the sofa. André in the armchair. Mr. and Mrs. Alexis took turns trying to draw me out, but it was clear they weren't interested. (How could you fail to be interested in a man who has pushed himself to your hearth?) At nine o'clock, they began to yawn.

First, Mr. Alexis yawned. And then Mrs. Alexis yawned. They yawned together, and then Mrs. Alexis yawned on her own. Andrée's mother yawned, and then the three of them yawned together. Mr. Alexis yawned three times in succession. Mrs. Alexis opened her mouth as if to yawn, and then the three of them rose from their places, put their hands over their mouths, and yawned.

It was the most alarming ritual I've ever witnessed.

I began to have serious doubts about my endeavor.

6. Defeat

That night, I sat up listening for their footsteps, acutely aware that the three of them could murder me whenever they wished. I didn't get a moment's sleep.

The following morning, the atmosphere had changed again. Andrée wasn't quite so friendly, and André was even less receptive. There was not a word exchanged at the breakfast table. Frankly, I felt insecure. I wondered what he'd told her, if he'd told her anything at all, and what she'd said. ("We can poison his eggs, darling.")

—André, I said, I think I'll come with you. I'd like to root around the city, see where you work. That okay?

He didn't answer, but it seemed to be okay. He drank his lukewarm coffee, then we went out together.

As soon as we were outside, he began:

—There isn't anything for you here. I don't know who wrote that letter, but you've got to be gone by six o'clock. You can't stay here.

I said:

—Listen, suppose you were homeless and friendless somewhere and the only person you knew was plowing your wife. Even if you hated him, you'd be pretty desperate for company, wouldn't you?

—I'm not plowing your wife.

—Listen, sure I'll go. Eventually. But what I don't understand is this business with Andrée. How could you fool around on your wife and your mother-in-law? I mean, I get the feeling you're pretty unscrupulous, so how come I'm evil and you're not? All I want is a place to stay.

We had reached the bus stop, and we were face-to-face. He looked at me as though he knew exactly where I was stretching the truth.

—You should be gone by six o'clock or no one will ever hear from you again.

And with that, as though our encounter had been scripted, he stepped onto the bus.

7. FURTHER DEFEAT

It wasn't possible to intimidate him, so my options were reduced. I would have to seduce Mrs. Alexis, eat a light meal, then leave by six o'clock. Unless, of course, Mrs. Alexis took my side against Mr. Alexis. That was always possible.

I walked around the city thinking about three things: Andrée, the time, and one of André's sentences:

—. . . no one will ever hear from you again.

The city itself was just what I needed: America, the flag everywhere, hoagies for breakfast, beavertails for lunch.

I went into a bookstore and bought *The Mountain and the Valley*, just in case Andrée was erotically fixated on this particular book. It was exactly as I remembered, almost completely without interest:

> As the train left the station, the couple in tweed began to relax. They exchanged a few words, in their American accent, and then, after a while, the man turned to me and . . .

Charmless prose, an unexciting story, predictable characters. Just the thing for young lovers. I resolved to use the direct approach.

When I returned to Newcastle Drive, Andrée answered the door, her face flushed, a white towel wrapped around her head, a terry-cloth robe held tight at her neck.

—Just in time, she said.

And again, her attitude had changed.

—Close the door. It's winter.

I closed the door and followed her into the living room, where she unwound the towel from her head and gave it to me.

—Dry my hair. If you don't mind . . .

Her mother was on the sofa, staring straight ahead. I took off my coat, draped it on the armchair, and took up the towel.

Andrée's hair was long. It fell to the middle of her back. Even wet, it was soft and smelled of lemon shampoo. I began to pat it dry, happy to perform this intimate service.

—Do the front, she said.

And turned to face me.

She stood inches from me, her robe slightly parted, her eyes looking directly into mine; my hands on her head, rubbing the towel this way and that. I had no idea what was going on, and to tell the truth, I was nervous.

—My mother tells me you're not André's friend at all. Never knew him in college; just met him the other day. That true?

(It was then I realized what bothered me about the old woman, aside from the gas I mean. When I'd first knocked at their door, she'd answered; she'd spoken to her daughter. If she was senile, it was a curiously selective dementia.)

—You came here to pay him back. How're you going to do that, Mr. Alexis? Are you going to hurt me?

I tried to move away, but she held me tight, holding her hips on mine, looking straight into my eyes.

—He did it with your wife, didn't he?

Her mother was staring at me, cheeks pink, hands in her lap. I didn't know where to look. The whole business was suddenly frightening. I pushed her away and made up my mind to leave.

Andrée followed me to my room.

—Not in here, she said. It's too clean . . .

I picked up my suitcase and fled.

8. Flight

I traveled east, hitchhiking.

From a car window, the towns I passed left meaningless impressions: here, a water tower was bright red; there, a farmhouse was black as cinder against the blue sky.

I was in shock.

9. The Sea! The Sea!

I was let off somewhere in Connecticut. It was night and cold, and the lights of the city were haloed. I could smell the ocean.

The stores had closed, and the center of town was abandoned. On Queen Street there was an all-night diner called The Horse's Asp. For six hours I sat there drinking coffee and eating orange crullers, and staring at my hands as though my fate were written on them. The people around me grew less and less genteel as the night went on until, at three o'clock, the place was filled with men who looked desolate under the fluorescent lights.

I was profoundly confused. Why had Andrée tried to seduce me? If André hadn't written the letter, who had? Who was in control, and what had my purpose been?

At three-thirty in the morning, I left The Horse's Asp, thinking about my murderer. (I was convinced I was about to die violently, and at that time, in that place, it seemed a good way to go.) I walked toward the sound of the ocean, following the soft yellow moon.

Despite the cold, I stood by the beach to admire the ocean's resolve, the way it beat its head against the shore. Then, no more than 100 feet away, a tall man, his back toward me, walked by with a narrow white bag on his shoulder. He didn't see me. He stopped, let go of the bag, and began to dig.

It was a winter night at the beach, so it was unusual that we were there together, immersed in our worlds, seeking the same solitude, as though we shared a misery. He was engaged in his private and obscure activity, unaware of me. But for his white bag, the only clearly visible part of him, I might well have walked on, believing myself alone. I felt then how peculiar God was, how strained His sense of humor. I began to walk toward the tall man, to offer my assistance.

At that moment, he turned and saw me approach. I was fifty feet away, but I could feel his panic. It was as though I'd frightened a rat. His face was obscure, but his whole body said fear. He ran from the beach. I ran a little way after him, to let him know how close I felt to his suffering, how much I wanted to help, but he ran that much faster, and he was in better shape than I. By the time I reached the place he had been, he was long gone, and he had left his white bag on the ground.

I had destroyed the brittle moment between us. I didn't know what to do with the bag, how to return it. I picked it up and dropped it and picked it up again. It was only when I decided to keep it as a memento that I realized there was something in it. The thing was cool and soft, a little wet, hard as cuttlefish in spots, yielding in others. For some reason, I thought it was a stuffed animal, but it was a human foot.

For a while I was confused. I thought: Why would you bury your own foot? It didn't occur to me that the foot was not his, that he'd run remarkably well without it. And how had he cut it off? Ax? Band saw? Circular saw? What kind of man carries a rotting foot around in a white bag and buries it on a beach where it's sure to be uncovered by the tide? Perhaps he'd hoped to bury it deep enough to preserve it until summer when, a stink amid the poorly dressed, it would cause havoc. Perhaps, perhaps . . .

No. I had no idea why he'd left the foot in the bag. It was beyond me. It was so completely beyond me that my faith in the existence of God was renewed, and my belief in the unsounded depths of human cruelty was revived.

Leaving the foot where it had fallen, I went away dazed. I kept to the walls or walked down the center of narrow streets so no one could surprise me. Only once was I startled: an animal ran out of Fred Martin's Sea Emporium and into an alley on the other side of the street.

10. RESTLESS

Naturally, some campaigns are more successful than others. I've discovered more ordered worlds on other excursions. (That and my depressions are what keep me going out.) This trip stays with me, though. First, because it began so forcefully before careening into defeat. Second, because I still wonder whose foot it was I'd held up. And, finally, because I still do not know who wrote the letter to Andrée that set me off.

If it wasn't André, it may have been Andrée. Lately, though, I'm convinced it was Andrée.

· IV ·

The Road to Santiago
de Compostela

minus these coincidences,
what is the world trying to tell me?
—BP NICHOL, *THE MARTYROLOGY, BOOK 4*

1.

In August, the landscape looked curiously white. The sun beat down on the fields and the houses. It bleached the spidery roads through France. Here and there on the way from Poitiers to Puente la Reina there were green fields, dirty villages, tin cities, and blue water. From the train, though, the chief impression was of white.

By the time it reached Bordeaux, there were travelers of different nationalities in every car. The Spanish names of their destinations were pronounced in a variety of ways: Estella, Santo Domingo, Sahagún, Santiago de Compostela ... They sounded romantic or vaguely sacred to the four Canadians who sat together in a bay reading, looking out the window, flipping through the pages of their pocket atlases.

—They run the bulls in Pamplona? said Mr. Lemoine. I wonder what that means?

He was facing his wife, but he spoke to no one in

particular. His wife looked up from her copy of *Mrs. Caldwell habla con su hijo*, a book she was trying to read in Spanish.

—What? she asked.

But Mr. Lemoine had already returned to the *Historical Guide to Aragón and Navarra*, his fingers poised on yet another photograph of yet another cathedral.

Sitting beside Mr. Lemoine was Mr. Davis, a young man with very little hair on his head, who wore red-framed sunglasses.

—Pamplona, said Mr. Davis, is where they set the bulls loose on the crowd.

—Set them loose? said Mrs. Lemoine.

—That's right. I was there one year when a couple of my traveling companions were gored. One of them died, but the other only got his buttock pierced.

—That's awful, said Mrs. Lemoine.

Mr. Davis pushed his glasses up and blinked.

—There's a few tourists dead every year. Americans mostly . . .

There was a moment's silence.

Mr. Davis took off his glasses, polished them, and nodded. Helen Strassberg, who sat facing him, rubbed her eyes and closed a copy of *Olivetti, Moulinex, Chaffoteau et Maury*, which she was trying to read in Catalan.

From what they could see of it, Bordeaux was homely. It was not even as attractive as Ottawa, the city they all came from. The Garonne passed slowly by, but it only inspired thoughts of home. (They had all been traveling just long enough to miss the pavilion by Dow's Lake, the pedal boats on the canal, the tulips by the Parkway, the Rideau at night.)

They were on their way to Santiago de Compostela, to visit Santiago cathedral, to acquire their *compostelana* and their scallop shells.

Miles of Europe went by, and then it was dark.

It was night, and the train swayed from side to side as if it were a boat. The clackety-click of the wheels was all that remained of solid ground. The lights were dimmed. You could see the moon and the stars from the windows. The Europeans, for whom it was getting late, began to curl up.

For the Canadians, it was afternoon. They tried to sleep. They read foreign newspapers and long books. They changed places, to make themselves comfortable: Mrs. Lemoine sat beside her husband; her husband sat by the window; Helen sat by the window with Mr. Davis beside her. They stretched out or curled up, but none of them could sleep.

And then, somewhere near midnight, Mr. Lemoine suggested it might be relaxing if each of them told a story about Love, or Ottawa, or Love in Ottawa.

As it was his suggestion, he began:

There was once a man who, without wishing to, fell periodically in love with the wife of his best friend's brother. It was an awkward passion, and it was particularly strong in spring. In fact, his passion existed *only* in spring. The rest of the year, he felt about Mrs. D'Amico much as he felt about everyone else: neutral. The rest of the year, he lived quietly with his mother who, discreetly, believed her son was homosexual. (Not that she would have minded. She was well read, and she had a fondness for Proust.)

For ten years Mr. Steiner's feelings grew. And then, in 1957, driven to the limits of desire, he declared himself. He said:

—You know, Mary, every year I have these feelings for you . . . especially in March . . .

Mrs. D'Amico understood this to be a compliment of some sort.

—Thank you very much, she said.

And she let the matter drop.

The following year, Mr. Steiner said:

—Listen, I still love you passionately . . . if you remember . . . Would you consider a sexual episode with me?

And again, Mrs. D'Amico was flattered and, truth be told, willing. She lived at 128 Blackburn with a brutish man with hair on his clavicle who was mentally cruel and sexually curt. So, from April 1 to June 20 that year Mr. Steiner and Mrs. D'Amico had passionate sex, the likes of which is rarely seen between humans. They rutted. They mated. They were conjugated in ways that Nature may not have intended. Mr. Steiner's mother would find them entwined beneath her chesterfield or submerged in her bathwater, and though she was delighted her son had finally discovered his libido, she was mortified by its chaotic expression. In their short time together, and largely unassisted by the literature, the lovers discovered nipple clamps, penis rings, and a jade statuette of a bald-headed monk that had once belonged to the Dowager Empress.

And then, at midnight on June 20, while Mr. Steiner was oiling up and Mrs. D'Amico was adjusting the rubber sheet on their bed, he lost all interest in her. He could no longer understand what purpose would be served by physical congress with Mrs. D'Amico. It was a devastating moment, made all the more humiliating by his efforts to continue as though he cared about what they were doing.

Naturally, there were tears and recriminations. Such pottery as could be found was flung; all to no avail. Their time had come. It took some fortitude for Mrs. D'Amico to return to her husband, but return she did. (Mr. D'Amico had barely noticed her absence, and her confession drove him to such frenzy he rolled up his newspaper and hit her with it.) Mr. Steiner, for his part, carried on as though everything were fine. And then, ten months later, he was as desperate for Mrs. D'Amico as he had been for eleven years.

And these were the beginnings of one of the most successful sexual relationships in history. (It was certainly the most successful in the nation's capital.) Each and every year, Mrs. D'Amico forgave him for his defective passion. And, each and every year, for three months, Mr. Steiner desired her as passionately as was humanly possible. They grew older. His mother died.

Her husband was struck by a bus. Until finally, in the spring of 1990, both of them in their eighties, they expired happily on the bed of their passions . . .

It was an unusual story, but it was followed by a friendly silence. Mr. Davis asked:

—Was this Steiner an M.P.? There was an M.P. from Carleton Place named Steiner . . .

—I don't think so, Mr. Lemoine answered.

—Still, said Mr. Davis, your average member of Parliament is a pretty strange bird . . .

It was an irrefutable observation. Each of them could recall an incident involving politicians who:

1. Had been found naked and dead on their office desks.
2. Had been seen to run naked through the halls of Parliament.
3. Often took advantage of parliamentary pages.
4. Often took advantage of constituents who wandered into their purview.
5. Were curiously labile.

It made you wonder about government. Was it redeemable? Could Canadians live without it?

Ms. Strassberg said:

—We could do without it if we were better than our politicians.

—There speaks an intellectual, said Mr. Davis.

—No, she's quite right! said Mrs. Lemoine. Just the

other day I was buying bread in the Market, and I swear a man just pushed me aside. Just like that! And I can tell you, because we know quite a few politicians, Frédéric and me, I can tell you no politician's going to push you down for a loaf of bread, I don't care what you say!

Mr. Lemoine turned the conversation to Prime Minister Trudeau. He had been quite arrogant in his day . . .

—Well, he was short, said Mr. Davis.

—But he was handsome, Helen said.

—Monsieur Trudeau wasn't so handsome, said Mrs. Lemoine. But he was a man.

—And Joe Clark wasn't a man? asked Mr. Davis.

—There's no comparison, said Mr. Lemoine.

—At least Clark didn't destroy the country . . .

It was matter for speculation just who *had* destroyed the country. The Lemoines were inclined to blame Mr. Mulroney, though, in Mr. Mulroney's defense, they agreed he was but one in a long line of wastrels. After John A. (alcoholic), there was Laurier (satyr) and Mackenzie King (psychotic). Diefenbaker was pug ugly, and John Turner was out of control. The rest were a motley crew of Bowells and Alexanders who had lined their pockets and died . . .

Finally, Helen said:

—Let's talk about something else.

The Europeans had curled up in their seats; their arms hung in the aisles or covered their brows. The darkness outside was broken only by an occasional star, by the platinum moon.

—Do you have a story? asked Mrs. Lemoine.

Helen said:

—I'm not very good at telling stories . . .

She told one, though:

Misha Bradley and Sharon Porter were born in Sandy Hill. Misha lived at 128 Russell and Sharon was one street over on Sweetland. They first met at L'Ecole Garneau where, as English children in a French school, they got along well, though even then Misha loved Sharon, while Sharon was confused by the sincerity of his feelings.

The years passed. Misha fell even more deeply in love. He couldn't sleep for dreaming of Sharon. He could barely eat. (His father had to threaten to call her parents before Misha would swallow anything at all.) And, of course, Sharon was aware of his state. He looked at her the way kittens look with their eyes closed. For twenty years he looked that way when he was near her. And, for most of those twenty years, she was a little cruel to him. She had him fetch her books or buy her candy, clean her room or wash her dishes.

Finally, after years of this, Sharon realized that Misha didn't *choose* to be cloying. He simply couldn't be otherwise around her, and his behavior brought out the worst in her. There was nothing they could do. So, on her twentieth birthday, she left home and traveled to the Far East. She studied Buddhism in India, and then in China, and finally in Japan, where she came to believe utterly in the Being of Nature, the truth of the present. She might even have remained in Japan for the rest of her life but, one night, during a long fast and while deep in meditation, she had a vision, and that vision was of Misha. She saw him clearly, as if he stood before her. He had aged, but he looked peaceful. And he stood still. Then, before her eyes, he became a willow, a willow with Misha's spirit. He grew from the lawn of her parents' home. He moved gently in the breeze, the blue sky tangled in his branches. It was the most beautiful thing she'd ever seen, and it was her destiny.

When she came out of her trance, Sharon got up without a word and returned home.

When they saw her, her parents wept with joy, and her friends came around constantly. But Misha was nowhere to be found. She learned to live in what was again a foreign city, and every morning she walked in Strathcona to admire the river and the trees.

And then, on her thirtieth birthday, Misha came home.

For ten years he'd worked in Gimli, Manitoba. And in all those years Misha had neither seen nor spoken to anyone from home (except, of course, his parents, to whom he wrote every week). Naturally, his feelings for Sharon had evolved. He had looked for her in other women: now living with a woman whose ears were like hers, now sleeping with a woman whose eyes were identical. In this way he came to believe he'd forgotten her.

But Misha's parents died, as all parents must, and he

returned home to discover that he and Sharon had been having an intense relationship during their years apart. They had lived with echoes of each other, and when they met again it was love.

They spent five wonderful days together.

And then, one night, as he was walking across the ice on the river, the ice gave out, Misha fell under, and his body was pulled along the Rideau to Billings Bridge, where it was discovered three days later.

Despite her life in the moment, Sharon's soul was razed.

On the day Misha's body was buried, she put a willow seedling in a clay pot, and the following summer, she planted it outside her front window.

For his part, Misha was deeply confused. His death was so unwelcome he refused to leave the earth. He wandered around the city looking for home. (His ghost was seen in Billings Bridge, in Ottawa East, and on campus at the University of Ottawa.)

Finally, a year later, Misha found Sharon's home on Sweetland, and that night, he appeared at the foot of her bed.

It wasn't a pleasant experience for either of them. By the time he reached her, Misha had forgotten why he'd come. He stood before her, looking like someone who'd lost his keys. When she moved, he moved with her, following her about the house wordlessly, and his soul gradually took up residence in the walls and floors.

As hauntings go, it was dull. It was what you'd

expect in Sandy Hill. At first, Sharon was pleasantly surprised. She made every effort to draw Misha out, to have him speak about death. But Misha was morose. Halfway between life and death, he had nothing to say about either. He simply followed her around the house, not very interested in anything at all.

After a while, Sharon began to miss her privacy. She also began to miss the Misha she'd known in life. The shade who followed her about had nothing to do with him. It was a soul that needed peace. (It felt nothing for her personally. It was the echo of a strong emotion.)

And so, six months after Misha's reappearance, Sharon painted every wall, floor, door, and ceiling in the house white. She painted her furniture white and what she could not paint she put in white boxes. She then began the tedious process of writing the words of the Bible on every surface.

From the kitchen ceiling ("In the beginning God created the heaven and the earth") to the last inch of the basement floor ("Woe be unto the pastors that destroy and scatter the sheep of my pasture!"), it took five years. She wrote the Bible over and over, hundreds of times. And when she was done, Misha did leave the house, but he took up residence in the willow she'd planted on the front lawn.

Over the years the tree grew, with Misha in its pith like smoke in a wooden canister. (On certain evenings you could hear him complain about the dead or the living, but he never left his tree.)

And though she was relieved to get him out of the house, Sharon was bitterly disappointed that the vision she'd had in Asia should come so literally true. Misha was a willow, but his willowness was off-putting.

Why should the gods go to such lengths to say so little?

They were even deeper into night, but they were in good spirits as they listened to Helen's voice.

—That was a good story, said Mrs. Lemoine.

Outside, it was not quite so dark. The moon was huge, and as they passed yet another river the water was a white tongue, the trees were black, and the stars looked dangerously sharp.

Mr. Davis took a flask of wine from the bag he had tucked beneath his seat.

—Should we? he asked.

—Why not? said Mr. Lemoine. Everyone is asleep. Where did you buy it?

—I bought it in Paris, before I got on the train.

Though he knew very little about wine, Mr. Lemoine took the bottle from Mr. Davis and squinted at the small print on the label.

Mrs. Lemoine said:

—Love *is* a mysterious thing . . .

Mr. Lemoine smiled.

—No, it's not mysterious. It's not any more mysterious than . . . platform shoes . . .

—But platform shoes *are* mysterious, said Mr. Davis.

—I mean it's an illusion . . .

—It's *not* an illusion, Helen said.

—Yes, but, watch out, eh? I don't mean it's a bad thing. It's a good illusion . . .

Mr. Davis handed each of them a foam cup. With the corkscrew of his Swiss Army knife, he opened the flask.

—Santé.

—Chin chin, said Mrs. Lemoine.

—Sex is the illusion, Helen said.

—Ah, no, said Mr. Lemoine. Sex is the real thing.

—It *is* a material fact, Mr. Davis said.

—I agree with Frédéric. You can time it. It must be real.

—No, said Helen, you mean coitus. That's not sex. Sex is push-up bras and prosthetic penises . . .

—I knew you were an intellectual, said Mr. Davis. You've done your research . . .

(It was the second time he'd mentioned her intellect as though it were something of which she should be ashamed. She was beginning to dislike him.)

—No, she's quite right, said Mr. Lemoine.

—So what is love?

—It's a state of mind . . . That's not the same as an illusion . . .

—Nuance, said Mr. Davis.

—Yes, nuance . . .

They drank from their cups.

—We're talking about the same thing, I think, Mr. Lemoine said gently. It's the things around coitus that are an illusion. A state of mind is a state of mind, okay. But some states of mind are better than others . . .

—No, Mr. Davis said. If you think like that, everything's a state of mind . . .

—Well, exactly . . . , Helen answered.

—Like love. Is love better than Florida?

—Florida?

—Florida is a state of mind when you're not in Florida.

—Oh, là il va trop loin, said Mrs. Lemoine.

Helen said:

—It isn't better than Florida, but it's better than Cornwall.

—I like Cornwall, said Mr. Lemoine.

And it was difficult to keep from laughing aloud, to keep from waking the men and women who slept in a chaos of linen and baggage.

—I have a story about love, Mrs. Lemoine said.

Maria de Cebreiro lived at 128 Florence, but every morning she walked to Notre Dame to pray. She would sit for hours, praying, staring at the altar until, gradually, the church faded from her consciousness. The church faded. The windows faded, and the stations of the cross disappeared, and Maria was left in a state of pious reverie, alone. This last stage of prayer, when she could hear the breath of Our Lord, was not always easy to attain. Sometimes it took as little as an hour. Sometimes it took as many as four, and it was not unusual to see Maria in her pew at the back of the church, deep in prayer.

When she was not in church, her life was a little

bland. She was poor, but fastidiously clean. All three of her dresses were black. She ate very little, and much of her time was taken up with reading. (She read the Bible because it was the word of God, *War and Peace* because it was long, and *The Stone Angel* because it was Canadian.) When she was not reading, she spent time with her sister Alicia.

Maria and Alicia were both in their sixties, but they were entirely different. Alicia, for instance, never set foot in church.

—Who cares if Saint Paul talks to the Corinthians or Thessalonians? she'd ask.

And then, on her sixty-first birthday, Maria was in Nôtre Dame contemplating the statue of the Virgin. It was as if she finally noticed the qualities of the sculpture: the blue of the firmament painted above, the dark brown head of the serpent beneath the Virgin's foot, the white of Mary's hood. And that day, the world seemed to disappear at once. Maria heard the footsteps of Our Lord, the rustling of His clothes. She tried to turn toward Him, to express her love, but it took forever to turn, though she could feel Him there, waiting in loving kindness.

For twelve hours, feeling nothing but the desire to see His face, she struggled in her mind to turn toward Him until, finally, she caught a glimpse of a face. It was an ordinary face, a face she'd known forever, though she was seeing it now for the first time, and she was suddenly aware of how beautiful faces were.

—Maria.

And again:

—Maria!

And she found herself on the cool floor of Nôtre Dame, a young woman standing above her, Father Scalasi by her side.

Now, an encounter like this would make anyone more observant of Heaven's will. Maria, though, devout as she already was, turned earthward. That is, she fell hopelessly, and carnally, in love with the face she'd seen.

It was a horrible thing to have happen so late in one's life, not because desire was unwelcome but because she was convinced she did not have the energy to survive it. She stopped eating. She couldn't sleep. She no longer went to church. She bought a long white dress and wore it around the house, wandering from room to room as if she were looking for a brush.

—Maria, her sister would say, stop pacing!

But Maria was distracted beyond distraction, and Alicia began to worry. In her mind, words like "addled," "softening," and "senile dementia" loomed. And, for a while, it did seem as if Maria had lost her bearings: three months after her vision, she took to the streets. She wandered along Bank much as she wandered at home in her white dress. Notre Dame was once again her destination, but she would find herself on unfamiliar streets in widely different parts of town.

Naturally, the impression she created was pitiful. Total strangers would lead her across busy streets and give her money for food. Hundreds of times a day, she heard:

—Are you okay, ma'am?

And she would answer:

—Yes, thank you so much . . .

It was clear to all concerned that *something* was wrong.

For months this was Maria's life: her white dress, a few bites of the dry sandwiches her sister forced her to eat, and a distracted effort to find Notre Dame.

And then, on a Monday in September, Maria found herself walking along Echo Drive, beside the canal. It was sunny, and the leaves had just begun to change color. The city was warm, it smelled of autumn, and the water looked clear and blue.

Maria had not eaten for days. Her head was light and she had trouble walking. One minute she was beside a large, redbrick house overlooking the canal; the next she was lying on the concrete promenade beside the canal itself, the sound of water in her ears. A voice said:

—Ça va-tu, ma chère? Savez-vous où vous êtes?

She looked up, and all she could see was the cloudless blue sky, then the tops of the houses, and finally the face of Mr. Richard Beaudoin. In Mr. Beaudoin's arms was a small Scottish terrier named Mireille.

—Vous vous êtes fait mal?

His face was kindly but narrow, with a shock of white hair that rose like a coxcomb on his skull. His eyes were unnaturally large behind his thick glasses. There was a thin, white mustache in a straight line beneath his nose. It was a good face, though homely, and it was nothing like the face of God. Still . . . his eyes were an almost transparent blue.

From the canal to her home on Florence, Maria was assisted by Mr. Beaudoin and his dog. She couldn't understand a word he said, in French or in English. She leaned on his somewhat unsteady frame, and thin as she was, it was enough.

How wonderful it would have been, had this been the beginning of love between them. It was no such thing. However grateful she felt to Mr. Beaudoin, and however often Mr. Beaudoin visited the sisters on Florence, Maria could not forget Our Lord's humble features. (It took nearly a year, but she *was* able to recover her senses, though she was haunted by her vision of God to the day she died.)

He works in mysterious ways, though. And it was Alicia who found something attractive in Mr. Beaudoin. She liked his ears, and she understood his accent. And, gradually, during his visits, they spoke less of Maria and more of things in general. Mr. Beaudoin's wife had died in the same year as Alicia's husband; not just the same year, the same month; not just the same month, the same day. They smiled sadly. Alicia put her hand on Mr. Beaudoin's arm and teased him about his eyes.

From that moment on, his visits were for her alone.

And when, a year later, he began to sleep over (at first, on the chesterfield with Mireille at his feet; and then, with Alicia, with Mireille on the floor), the three of them would rise early in the morning. Then Richard and Alicia would walk Maria to Notre Dame for morning mass.

—That's a good story, said Mr. Lemoine. But isn't it about Hélène Proulx?

It was two in the morning. Without quite meaning to, they had finished Mr. Davis's wine.

—Yes, Mrs. Lemoine answered.

—She lived in Sandy Hill, didn't she?

—I changed it . . .

Helen said:

—I used to live in Sandy Hill, when I was at U of O. On Templeton.

—And what did you study? asked Mrs. Lemoine.

Mr. Davis interrupted:

—My favorite part of town is Ottawa West or Woodroffe or Brittania, somewhere near the river . . .

—Ottawa's not such a great city, said Mr. Lemoine.

But just before he did, Helen said:

—Sociology.

And Mr. Davis spoke of his childhood.

—When the Beach Boys were really popular, I begged my parents for a surfboard. Everybody had a surfboard. There were kids surfing on the canal, but we tried to surf the rapids near the Champlain Bridge . . . It's amazing we weren't killed.

—It's no Montréal, Mr. Lemoine continued.

—Thank God, Mrs. Lemoine said. Every two minutes there's somebody killed in Montréal.

—I like Montréal, said Helen.

—I like Toronto, Mr. Davis said.

His companions stared at him. Mr. Lemoine asked:

—Why?

—I'm not saying I would live there, okay. But it's good place to visit . . .

Mrs. Lemoine said:

—Oh, well, what's the difference anyway?

—There's one difference, said Mr. Davis. In Toronto, the police only shoot black people. In Montreal, they shoot black people, white people, and domestic animals.

—And it's all by accident, said Mr. Lemoine.

—It's all accidental . . .

And it was suddenly, vividly, as if they hadn't left home. Europe vanished. (It was somewhere beneath the soft darkness outside.)

Mr. Davis yawned.

—I'm getting tired, he said. I better tell my story before we fall asleep . . .

The M'Kolos lived at 128 Herridge, in Ottawa East. It was rumored that they'd been cannibals "back where they came from," but, as with all such rumors, this was something of an exaggeration. The M'Kolos had "come from" Glencoe, which is not known for its man-eaters, and in all their lives they knew only one cannibal. In every way but this, they were a typical Canadian family, or tried to be.

Of course, the cannibal in question was Mr. M'Kolo's great-grandfather, Thomas, who lived with them. He was not a member of a tribe of noble warriors who ate their enemies out of respect. He was merely insane. The M'Kolos were of African descent, but most of the flesh Thomas had eaten was that of a woman from Glencoe named Judith Hannah.

It was a vexing situation. The M'Kolos genuinely loved and revered Mr. M'Kolo Senior. They also believed him to be a god, and not without reason, either: in his lucid moments, the elder M'Kolo could change lead into gold with his bare hands. He could predict the future with complete accuracy, and his breath revived their houseplants.

The M'Kolos kept him locked up in the basements of their various houses, and after one of their infants was eaten, they kept their children away from him as well.

(The maiming of their daughter, Catherine, and the death of the woman from Glencoe were unfortunate accidents. Catherine, two years old, had toddled too close to the bars of her great-great-grandfather's cell, and before they stopped him, he had eaten one of the child's arms and part of her left leg. The woman from Glencoe had been a meter reader. The M'Kolos didn't even realize she'd been eaten until the gas company called two weeks later to ask if they'd seen her. It was shortly thereafter that the M'Kolos left Glencoe.)

Despite the elder M'Kolo's gifts, the family lived modestly. There was no way to predict when he would regain his sanity or how long he would remain lucid. They kept mounds of lead beside his cell, along with a sheet of questions about the future:

.   .   .

1. Who will win the Grey Cup?
2. Which stock will rise highest in the coming year?
3. How much will our house be worth by the end of April?

And so on . . . In this way, they made enough money to sustain them for a year or two at a time. (They dispersed their gold on the black market. They bought and sold shares in successful enterprises. They paid their property taxes.)

Nor did they have to maintain or feed the elder M'Kolo. He seemed to live on the air in his cell, or on the small animals that wandered into his reach. In almost every way, he was worth the risk.

And then, in 1987, something unusual happened. On January 15 Thomas M'Kolo regained his senses, and he remained lucid for three whole months, months during which, though they kept him in his cell, the family ate downstairs, near him, together. He was ecstatic. He tended to the houseplants. He turned so much lead into gold they could barely hide it all.

Then, on the night of March 14, the elder M'Kolo called his great-grandson to his cell. It was late. His wife and their daughters were asleep, but Mr. M'Kolo went down to his great-grandfather.

The elder M'Kolo seemed to be in good spirits, but he said:

—This isn't going to be a good year for you, M'Kolo.

He said it so spitefully, his great-grandson drew back.

—Your wife and two of your daughters are going to die.

—How?

—Three ways: diphtheria, a ruptured appendix, a ruptured spleen . . .

And because he loved his wife and his daughters, Mr. M'Kolo took the news badly. He wept. He wept because his great-grandfather was never wrong about the future, and in his mind a door shut and there was silence.

—Isn't there anything I can do?

—It will mean a sacrifice . . .

—I'll do anything.

—Good. Here's what you do: on the 15th of September come down here, unlock my cell, and sleep beside me . . .

Then the elder M'Kolo began to speak Farsi, and he was gone.

But what a dilemma he left with Mr. M'Kolo: death or the death of those he loved. He didn't speak of his misery, but for six months he prepared for his own demise.

He wasn't the least surprised when, at midnight on the 14th of September, his wife contracted diphtheria, Sonya's appendix burst, and Judith fell from her chair and ruptured her spleen.

After drinking a bottle of Hudson's Bay Vodka, he went down to his great-grandfather's cell, opened the door, and went in.

It wasn't at all what he expected. He was in a vast desert in white sunlight. The dunes went on forever. Not three feet from him, a black river ran. Beside the river, his great-grandfather stood naked, his eyes closed. Without a word the elder M'Kolo advanced and took him by the throat. He held him and squeezed, and Mr. M'Kolo felt the life go out of him. It seemed to take years to lose consciousness, years during which he struggled with and sometimes even overpowered his great-grandfather, but he lost consciousness.

When he awoke, minutes later, he was surprised to find himself intact, his body whole. He was in the elder M'Kolo's cell, and it smelled as it usually smelled, of the close. There was no desert, no river, no sunlight. His great-grandfather was gone, but there were other voices in his mind.

He called out to his wife, but instead Sonya came downstairs. She was older and gray-haired, but he could see she was his daughter. She smelled curiously good.

—Your appendix really needed attention, didn't it? he asked.

She smiled.

—Will you just touch these for me, Dad?

With a stick she pushed a mound of lead toward him.

In an instant he saw how great his sacrifice had been. There wasn't much time. He touched the lead. It turned to gold, of course. And he clearly saw that it would be at least a hundred years before he died. In anger, he cried out. He called for his wife; he cursed his great-grandfather, but he was speaking Farsi, and then he was gone.

. . .

—How do you expect us to sleep after that? asked Mrs. Lemoine.

Mr. Davis smiled.

—It wasn't so bad, was it?

No, it was only a story, but he had told it well, so they were silent for a few minutes, while the train rocked from side to side and clickety-clacked, and the sound of snoring reached them as though from a distant turbine.

—Was that about love or about Ottawa? asked Mr. Lemoine.

—Both, answered Mr. Davis.

—More about God, though, said Helen.

—Don't get started about God, Mrs. Lemoine said.

But it was too late. Mr. Davis said:

—It wasn't about God.

—Why not?

—Well, God doesn't speak. So, Mr. M'Kolo can't be God.

—He speaks in the Bible, Helen said.

—You mean the burning bush? A bush can't speak. He just set fire to the thing while he was in Moses' mind, that's all . . .

—I guess that's why silence is golden, Mr. Lemoine concluded.

Mr. Davis continued:

—All *we* can do is not talk. It's not the same . . .

—That's just nonsense, Helen said.

—You see? said Mrs. Lemoine. If you start talking about God it never stops . . .

—It's not so complicated, said Mr. Lemoine.

—But is it true? Helen asked.

Mr. Davis answered:

—Sure it's true. Try to keep quiet, see if your brain doesn't go on and on . . .

—So, in God's mind nothing happens? asked Mr. Lemoine.

—He doesn't have a mind. Silence doesn't have a . . .

—The Zen Buddhists can be silent, said Helen. When they meditate, they say they're not thinking about anything . . .

—But there's still their bodies. I don't even know if their minds are quiet, but their bodies aren't.

—Please, let's not talk about it, said Mrs. Lemoine. God is God or He isn't God. It doesn't matter. There's so many better things to talk about . . .

—Okay, okay, but I think the real essence of human nature is noise. That's my philosophy.

—Noise? asked Mr. Lemoine.

—Noise. Like talk . . . It's very fancy and everything, but it's just the noise you make, that's all. You can't help it. Born crying; dead whining . . .

Helen yawned.

—I think you're using the word "silence" in your own way, she said. You could just as easily say God speaks a language we don't understand, and that all our noise, as you call it, is the only real silence . . . Cows moo, you know . . .

—I don't think you understand, said Mr. Davis.

—I think I do.

—Then I suppose you're right, he said.

Without a shred of conviction.

They were all, now, mercifully, tired.

Helen watched her companions nod off. Mr. Lemoine pulled his jacket over his shoulder, and, his head against the window, drew his wife to him, his arm around her shoulder, her head on his chest. They were asleep in no time.

Helen and Mr. Davis went on talking about this and that, but they were acutely aware of their differences. He seemed to genuinely resent her intelligence and tried to engage her in a conversation about cooking. It was a relief to both of them when he managed to fall asleep somewhere around five o'clock in the morning, which was somewhere around eleven o'clock in Ottawa.

—What a creep, Helen thought.

Before she herself fell asleep, the bits and pieces of the day returned: the world under white sunlight, the Dowager Empress, countless rivers and fields, the voices of her compatriots . . . English, English, French, French . . . and what was that about God? . . . As if there weren't silences enough to fill an arena: her silence now, her silence listening, her silence waiting, the silence of a field, the silence of a field in winter, the silence of the train, which was her silence as if she were the train . . . Mr. Davis's face, his voice . . . Back home it was night . . . The rivers were black and smooth as they bled through the city . . . The clock on the Peace Tower rang softly: one, two, three, four . . . and she could suddenly hear it, because she had reached the place where Santiago de Compostela is a suburb of Ottawa, and Ottawa a suburb of Santiago, a suburb of Pamplona, of Paris, of St. Petersburg ... All one in God, they say ...

And then she fell asleep, her mother's hand in hers as they crossed the Laurier Bridge on the way home.

ACKNOWLEDGMENTS

Grateful acknowledgment is made to the following for permission to reprint from previously published material:

"Despair" and "The Third Terrace" were first published in slightly different form in *Event* magazine. "Horse" was first published in *Ambit*.

Quotes by Francis Ponge in "The Third Terrace" are from: *Pieces,* (Paris: Gallimard, 1962).
Quotes in "Horse" are from: Fernando Pessoa (Portuguese) and Guillaume Apollinaire (French).

Lyrics from "Congo Man," written by S. Francisco. © Ice Records. All rights reserved. Used by permission.